KALI KUSAIN
COUNTERFEIT QUEEN

KYEATE

Kali Kusain

Copyright © 2018 by Kyeate

Published by Mz. Lady P Presents

All rights reserved

www.mzladypresents.com

This book is a work of fiction. Names, characters, places, and incidents either are the product of the author's imagination or are used fictitiously and are not to be construed as real. Any resemblance to actual persons, living or dead, business establishments, events, or locales or, is entirely coincidental

ACKNOWLEDGMENTS

J.A.Z- my three amigos, thank you guys for allowing mommy to be an inspiration for your future endeavors and school projects. You guys are my everything

My grandparents, Liz, and Stacey thanks for being the best to ever do it period. I can't thank y'all enough. My ass will be thanking you in every book I ever write, lol.

My bestie westie: Meagan Huff, girl thank you for being the best friend a girl could ask for. Thank you for listening to my crazy ideas when I discuss a book with you and all of the support that you give when I don't even ask for it. I promise if I ever make it big, you coming along for this ride my girl!

I just want to acknowledge my pen sisters of MLLP. If y'all don't know by now I love y'all.

Mz. Lady P: I thank you for being you and giving me a chance to spread these wings of mine. I never knew that I would come this far. Thank you for the teaching experiences and let me showcase my talent.

My big sister, Trenae: thank you for all the encouraging words and seeing potential in me. You just don't know how much that means to me.

I would like to thank the following people for the continual support Zatasha, Dedra B., Shaye B., Quita Martin, MsMolly Lovin-Niya, Maria Robles, and She'na Flowers. I'm trying to think of everyone off the dome right now, so if I forgot you, it wasn't intentional.

Brandi Jefferson, my lovely editor, if you aren't the sweetest person ever. I thank you for the motivation and pointers that you give. I love the fact that you are hands-on and tell your thoughts. You make it fun and a learning experience. Keep up the great work because you are a beast at what you do.

For everyone that has ever dreamed of something, stop doubting yourself. I doubted myself for so many years, and I just think about where I could be now if I hadn't of doubted myself. I'm happy with the process that I have taken, and I'm just going to continue to ride out this wave. Anything you dream, you can achieve.

To all my readers as always, I can't thank you guys enough for all the support. I will do my part by continuing to have something for you to read. I would also like to thank all of those that have given me a try by reading my work. You guys make this fun. I love the interactions and the messages. I love when my story can connect and have a change in someone's life.

If I have the product and the drive, I will continue to thrive. Never slacking on my pimping, I got whatever you need. One love from me ~ The Pen Madame Kyeate.

STAY CONNECTED

Facebook: Author Kyeate / Kyeate Holt
    Facebook: Kyeate's Book Club
    Instagram: Kyewritez
    Twitter: Adjustnmykrown
    Website: www.authorkyeate.com
    I love to interact and engage with my readers so feel free to hit me up and follow me if you don't already.
    All books are available on Amazon and Kindle. For my local readers, you can also find my books in the local Nashville libraries.

CHAPTER 1

Walking down the long hallway, my Manolo Blahnik heels were smoking as my pace picked up the closer I got to this meeting. This warehouse was one of many that I had. The smell of printed money made my nipples hard. I walked into the room, and my crew was already seated waiting for me. It was almost midnight, and I was pissed that I had to get up out of my plush California King bed because somebody wanted to cross me. I removed my shades and laid them on the table.

"Kali, why the hell you call a meeting this late?" my brother Kalicio huffed. The way I looked at him, if he weren't family, I would've shot his ass in the head.

"Kalicio, when I open my mouth to speak, you will be addressed, until then, don't fucking question me about shit!" I yelled. I placed both of my hands on the table and held my head down.

"Now somebody please tell me the main rule on how I run my shit?" I hissed. I lifted my head, and everyone was looking around at each other as if they ain't heard what the hell I just said.

"That was a motherfucking question! Any other time everyone seems to be so talkative!" I yelled. Kalicio leaned forward and whispered in my ear

"Yo, what the hell is going on?" he questioned. I held my hand up to hush him.

"Somebody better answer my question or every last one of y'all can say goodbye to a job," I said in a calmer tone.

"No using money with any other organizations because they're already buying from us," one of my younger workers spoke up. I clapped my hands.

"Thank you, so why in the hell did I receive a phone call from my dear friend about some fishy shit from one of my workers?" I asked looking at the person who I knew was responsible.

I ran the biggest counterfeit money ring in the south. My shit was legit and untraceable. I picked up my learning tactics from the best to ever do it straight from Lima, Peru. In order to keep my business running smoothly, my main rule was if you had any dealings with another organization, especially ones that I dealt with, no counterfeit bills were supposed to be used.

"Man, it was an accident I grabbed the wrong wallet," Chris spoke up.

Kalicio turned around to look at Chris. My brother was the tamer one at times. He was a big ass teddy bear to me, but to everyone else, they wouldn't dare look at him wrong. Kalicio was the baby at twenty-five. I was the oldest at thirty. Kalicio stood six feet four and weighed about a good three hundred pounds. He was the color of hazelnut coffee creamer and rocked a jet-black beard that matched his low cut fade. That was our Kusain blood running deep.

"Chill, Kalicio. Chris, I want to believe you, but if it were an accident, you would've corrected the issue, right? You left, and then I had to get a damn phone call," I spoke in a calmer tone.

I was trying to remain calm even though I wanted to knock this nigga into the middle of next week. If I showed that Kalicio would act on it, and I couldn't have that. Chris sat there looking dumbfounded.

"Chris, I'm putting you back on warehouse detail until I see otherwise. If your mother weren't in the middle of chemo treatments, I would fire your little ass," I told him.

Kalicio shook his head. I would deal with him later.

"If anybody else decides to pull some shit like that again, I'm not going to be so nice. Now go the fuck home!" I yelled.

Everyone cleared out and went on about their business. I grabbed my shades and placed them back on my face.

"KK, why you always got to talk to a nigga like I ain't shit in front of them niggas? I'm supposed to be your right hand, your fucking brother, and you steady disrespecting me. That shit ain't cool," Kalicio asked. I hated when he acted like this. This was him being the baby.

"Kalicio, at the end of the day this is my business. You still work for me. I must handle things accordingly. I'm not going to come to you with every problem. If I needed your help, you would've been the person I came to. Not everything is going to come pass you, and it's not that I don't respect you, but this is my concern. I like the peace I have in the streets amongst others, and I want to keep it that way. Do I come to you and try to tell you how to run what you got going on?" I asked.

Kalicio stood up and walked towards to me. He towered over me with his big ass. He leaned down and kissed my forehead.

"It's all good, little sis. You right I was tripping. I'm about to head out. Breakfast in the morning?" he asked.

"Let's try lunch, I need some rest," I told him. Kalicio nodded his head, and I watched him walk out.

I walked upstairs to my office that overlooked the floor and watched my overnight workers do what they did best. This was always an extreme high for me. Money period gave me a feeling that no one could give me. My brother and I struggled so much as kids that I vowed I would never be broke again if I had anything to do with it. When people looked at me, they would never think I was the queen of the biggest fucking scandal in the south. I don't want to toot my own horn and come off as big headed, but I was a bad bitch. With my father being Peruvian and my mother being Dominican, my looks was that of an exotic supermodel. I wasn't the supermodel type though. I stood about five feet three and weighed one hundred seventy pounds. My curves were enough to make one dizzy, and I loved it.

As I said growing up, Kalicio and I didn't have it easy. We were born in the states, but then we were shipped back to Lima, Peru to live with our father when our mother passed. We lived in one of the most dangerous parts of Lima, Peru. San Juan de Lurigancho wasn't the most pleasant parts to grow up in. Some of the things we saw made Kalicio and I have the tough exteriors we had now. With us being Americans, they were hard on us behind my father's back. They wouldn't dare disrespect my father in his face. We stayed there for two years until my father up and decided to send us back to the states. I think raising kids wasn't his forte. It was Kalicio and I looking out for each other. Most of the times Kalicio looked up to me as a mother figure since I was five years older than he was. When that nigga hit a growth spurt, he thought he was my daddy.

"Kali," the voice of a female broke me from my thoughts. I turned around and locked eyes with my night shift manager, Myia. I didn't really fool with many females, but Myia had been down since day one. She was Kalicio's main chick.

"Wassup, Myia?" I asked.

"Is everything good, I seen you staring down like you was mad about something?" she asked. I wasn't about to tell her what was going on, and it was no reason for me to be rude and smug towards her.

"I'm fine. I was just stuck in a daze and thinking. You know sometimes I space out," I reassured her. My phone buzzed. I looked down at the incoming text.

Feel Good: Man: Where u at? A nigga's been sitting out here since we left the meeting.

Me: Omw

I looked up at Myia and made my way towards the door.

"I'm about to head out. Is everything straight on the floor?" I inquired. Myia nodded her head.

"You know I got everything covered. Go home and get you some rest," Myia said. I placed my shades back on my face and headed out of the warehouse.

Walking out of the warehouse, I jumped in my Wraith and headed home. Looking at the time on the dash, it was almost two in the morning. Seeing that I had to come out and take care of business so late, I was grumpy because I needed my beauty sleep. It was going to take me at least another twenty minutes to get home.

I turned the volume up and jammed to the sounds of NBA Youngboy. I knew the little piece I had waiting was going to be mad, but he knew what the hell was up and him speaking on anything regarding me would have his ass cut off in the quickness. I was single and didn't have much time for a man, but it wasn't nothing wrong with getting my back blown out.

I pulled into the driveway of my mini-mansion. It was just me, so I splurged on other things. People would laugh at me because I still had six bedrooms and four baths talking bout what was mini about that. I stepped out the car, and there he stood waiting on me like the perfect watchdog. Canton stood there with his hands in his pockets. He hovered over me in height, and his dark chocolate skin was even perfect in the dark.

"A nigga was about to leave," he whispered, placing a kiss on my neck. His lips sent a wave through me.

"Well that shit needed to be addressed and afterwards I talked with Myia for a few," I told him, breaking his embrace.

We entered my home, and I sat the alarm. After that, I sent a notification to my guards that I was in for the night. I had to have security detail out the ass because being a female in the game I was in, I was a target at times.

KALICIO

I couldn't get my mind off the meeting the whole drive to my bitch's house. I wasn't even bothered by the little shit Chris pulled. Kali motherfucking ass be talking to a nigga like I'm her damn child. The level of disrespect was getting out of hand. Don't get me wrong. I love my sister with all my heart. I always looked up to her like a mother, but seeing her running something that I should be running had a nigga feeling some type of way.

I had my hands in other shit, and that was in drugs. If I couldn't be the boss of Kali's shit, then I was going to be the boss of my own shit. I had a little crew ready to put in work. I just needed to link up with the right connect.

I pulled up in Dodge City. I had a little piece over here that I dicked down on occasion. If Myia's ass knew I was stepping out on her, she would kill a nigga. I couldn't resist though. When I came over here, I made sure I drove one of my chill cars and dressed down. These niggas were vultures over here, and I couldn't be caught slipping. I hopped out the Dodge Ram truck that I was in making sure that I was strapped. I adjusted my shirt and made my way through the bricks and to my destination.

I could hear loud talking and laughing through the door, and I bit down on my bottom lip. This bitch knew when I came over her shit was supposed to be cleared the hell out. I don't like motherfuckers in my business, and damn sholl don't like no stranger sitting up in my fucking face. With my fist balled up, I started to beat on the door like the damn police. It didn't take much from my big ass. With my three hundred pound frame, I damn near knocked the door down.

"Who the fuck is beating on my door like they the damn police?" Ju yelled.

The door swung opened, and when she saw me, her facial expression went from angry to calm. I looked at her without saying a word, and she already knew what time it was.

"Ok, y'all it's time to go. I'll hit y'all later," she told her little ratchet crew. The many damn different colors of weave in this bitch had it looking like a bag of Skittles.

I leaned against the wall as they all scattered like roaches. Once the coast was clear, I made my way inside. This hoe better be glad, I'm trying to link up with her brother so I can get plugged.

"What the fuck I tell you about having motherfuckers over here when I show up? If you can't follow simple directions, then you gone be cut off July!" I spat. Yes, her name was July, and it was her government. Her motherfucking birthday was in December with a July name.

"Kalicio, you didn't have to be so rude though. Them were my friends." She pouted. I removed my hat and placed it on the table.

"Them hoes helping you pay the rent in this shit? Did them hoes help you when your lights were off last week? Why the fuck you still staying in the projects? I know your brother done offered to move your ass!" I spat. Ju rolled her eyes.

"I don't like asking him for help. I'm fine staying right here. How long you staying tonight?" she asked.

A nigga didn't want to answer because I really planned on dicking her down, mentioning her brother, and then getting ghost. Myia ass would be rolling in about five a.m., so I knew I had to beat her home.

"Just come over here and take care of me," I said, licking my lips.

July might have been ratchet, but her body was banging as hell. She had an ass out this world that was all natural. She was young with no kids, so them titties were still perky. She was the perfect bitch until she opens her mouth. July made her way over to me and squatted down between my legs.

"I talked to my brother," she teased while tugging the string on my pants. *Bingo!* That was what I wanted to hear.

"You did. What he say?" I whispered while caressing her face putting it on thick.

"He said you could meet him tomorrow. He will be at the shop at noon," she said.

I nodded my head and pulled my dick out so that she could show me what that mouth do. I watched as July braided her hair and wrapped that shit up in some type of shit on her head. She placed her plump lips around the tip of my shit and started going to work. I closed my eyes and rested my head on the back of the couch. July would give Superhead a run for her money. My phone started ringing and I reached for it and looked at the screen Myia ass was calling. I tapped the top of July head so that she could stop.

"What the fuck, Kalicio!" she yelled. I placed my hand to my mouth signaling for her to shut up.

"Hello," I said in the phone.

"Why you not at the house?" Myia blew into the phone.

It seems like soon as I answered the phone Ju's ass went back to sucking. A nigga couldn't control himself, and I felt myself about to punch her in her shit.

"I had to make a quick stop. I'll be there in about five minutes," I told her trying to make sure my voice was steady and regular.

"Whatever, Kalicio!" she spat and hung up the phone. Fuck! I looked at the phone and put it in my pocket. Ju was still on her knees, and she had a full-blown attitude. I gave zero fucks.

"Get up, I gotta go," I said, standing up and fixing my pants. Ju sucked her teeth.

"How you gone cut my time short just because she calls?" she asked. I looked at her as if she had two heads.

"Girl, I don't owe you no explanation. You know this here is straight fun, nothing else. When my woman calls I don't care what it is I'm doing, I go," I told her. Shit, plus a nigga didn't feel like dealing with Myia's crazy ass. She was just about as crazy as KK, and that's why they asses clicked like they did.

I knew I had to keep Ju happy at least until I linked with her brother. She could easily call that nigga and speak ill on my name. I reached into my pocket and pulled out a wad of cash. I don't even know how much it was, but I gave it to her.

"You know I will make it up to you," I told her kissing her on the cheek. I left her apartment and headed back to my truck so that I can take my ass home.

When I pulled up outside of the house, I sat in the truck for a moment. I grabbed the blunt from behind my ear and lit it up. I needed to ease my mind and say a prayer. I prayed that when I stepped foot in this house that Myia's ass wouldn't try to fight. After taking a couple of tokes, I put the blunt out and headed inside.

Walking into the house, it was dark as fuck. I could barely see trying to make my way to the steps. My ass tripped missing the bottom step.

"If you were already home when I got here you wouldn't be about to bust your ass!" Myia spat. I sighed and used my phone to light the steps so that I could see.

"What the hell wrong with you? Damn, did KK snap on your ass at the warehouse, why you home so early anyway?" I questioned.

Miya stood at the top of the stairs with her hands on her hips. I loved to see her mad. Myia was beautiful, and she was made for me. I was a big nigga, so I had to have me a nice sized woman. Myia was what folks considered a BBW. She had the biggest breasts and the hips to match. I loved her body and the curves that came along with it. Her stomach wasn't fat nor was it toned, but I loved to kiss on it because it was mine. I headed towards the bedroom, and Myia was on my heels. I started to remove my jewelry and placed it on the dresser.

"You better pray that soon as you connect with this motherfucker Premium that you cut that hoe July off!" she spat with so much venom.

What really fucked me up was that how in the hell did she know about July. A nigga was extra careful; at least I thought I was.

"Don't even open your mouth to lie. I may be cooped up in that warehouse all the time, but I know what the fuck is going in my house. So, what little fun you been having, dead that shit otherwise you will see a side of me that you don't like," she calmly said.

I didn't even have a comeback. She removed her robe and got in bed like a nigga wasn't even there. I hated that cold shoulder shit. I removed my clothes and hopped in the shower washing today off me, hoping that tomorrow everything goes well with Premium.

KALI

"Do that shit, Canton," I moaned. Canton had his head planted deep between my thighs. We had been going at it all night. Canton was a beast in the bed, and that's what I kept him around for. We didn't do the feelings thing, nor was commitment on our agenda. I knew that it most definitely wasn't on mine. I placed my hands on Canton's head pushing him deeper into my pussy because I was about to wet his face up. Canton kept his tongue right there on my spot, and I came all on his face. I laid there getting myself together.

I looked at the clock, and it was almost noon. Shit, I forgot I'm supposed to be having lunch with Kalicio. Sitting up, I grabbed my phone off the nightstand. Checking over a few texts, I saw that Kalicio pushed lunch back because he had something to do. I rolled my eyes and threw the phone on the bed. Canton walked back in the room with a towel around his waist. He looked a little too comfortable to me. For some reason, and it never failed after I got my nut, I wasn't for all that lingering around. Get the fuck out was my motto.

I swung my feet over the side of the bed and slid them in my slippers. Grabbing my robe off the chaise, I put it on and headed to the bathroom so that I can shower.

The door to the bathroom crept opened, and I turned to face the door. Canton was standing there fully dressed.

"I'm about to head out. That shipment comes in today, and I'll oversee it unless you want to do it?" he asked. Turning the water off, I opened the door, and Canton handed me my towel.

"You can go ahead. I might be running a little behind today," I told him.

Canton was one of my workers. If I trusted anybody with anything, besides Myia, it would be him. Not because he was good in bed, but his work ethic was impeccable. Canton nodded his head and left out the bathroom.

Walking into my walk-in closet, I pulled out my royal blue Balmain t-shirt and a pair of cut up shorts. I was going to rock this with my royal blue thigh high boots. I never half-stepped, whenever you saw me, I was dressed to impress and all about my paper. Once I got dressed, I grabbed my phone and headed downstairs.

The aroma coming from the kitchen made my stomach growl. Marisol, my in-house maid, knew what she was doing. When I entered the kitchen, Marisol stood there talking to her son, who was one of my security detail.

"Marisol, is that Tacacho I smell?" I asked.

Tacacho was one of my favorite foods from back home. It was a dish back home that we ate for breakfast, which consisted of plantains and pork combined in a ball served on a bed of rice. Marisol handed me a plate and a smile graced my face.

"Muchas gracias, te lo agradezeco mucho (thank you so much, I really appreciate it)," I told her. Marisol smiled.

"Senorita, you been working on your Spanish?" she asked.

Marisol would be walking around here speaking Spanish, and it would piss me off because my shit was rusty as hell. When I took trips to Peru, the people I dealt with knew to speak English around me and nothing else.

"I've been doing a little something, something," I laughed. I tore down that food as if it was my last meal.

While I sat at the table, I pulled up the cameras on my iPad and checked in at the warehouse. Things looked to be moving smoothly. Shipment should be arriving within an hour. I had new plates, ink, and bonded paper coming straight from Peru. People paid top dollar for our sheets because they were that untraceable. I had about twenty-four people working in the warehouse because to get the bill done right it took ten to twelve people with each being assigned a task. It took us about a week to make five million dollars, so with the extra people, we were able to produce more and send it out. That's why I had Myia running night shifts because that was when production took place due to the machines being loud.

With the shit I did, if I were ever caught, I probably would never see the light of day. That's why I was careful who I worked with and was adamant about not crossing other crews. It will only take one rat to bring down my organization with uncalled for beef.

Kalicio

SITTING OUTSIDE of Premium's shop, I had arrived a little early just so that I could peep the scene. Premium was a big-time plug, and I needed him so that I could get some proper work. I checked my watch, and it was ten minutes until noon. I got out of the truck and made my way towards the entrance of the shop. As I approached, I was immediately stopped by a nigga who was the same size as me. I was in another man territory, but I was far from a bitch.

"I need to search you, my man," he said, stepping towards me.

I rolled my eyes and held my hands up. I ain't have shit on me anyway. Once he was done, he opened the door to the shop, and another guy met me.

"Follow me," he stated.

I nodded my head and followed him through the barbershop into the back. We hit the corner, and I was led into a room. Premium had his back to me when I entered the room.

"I see you on time. I like a man who shows dedication and make good on first impressions. I even like how you peeped the scene because you didn't know what you were coming into," Premium stated. I nodded my head and took a seat in front of him.

Premium was a skinny nigga, but size didn't mean shit. His name rang bells in these streets like Kali's did.

"So, you know I had to ask myself why my sister stuck her neck out for a nigga. I said it had to be somebody she really fucked with. I told her it would come back on her if things ever got bad. So, you fuck with my sister?" Premium asked. This nigga just had to go and bring July ass up.

"Look, I'm gonna keep it all the way funky with you. I got a woman, and Ju knows about her. Ju also knows that this thing we got going on is just for fun. Nevertheless, I also look out for her, and she knows that. As far as me and Ju being serious, I don't see myself leaving my girl because she a real one," I told him hoping that I didn't fuck up my chances.

"One thing about July, she ain't ever been the one to listen. So please keep y'all personal shit away from my business," he stated.

"Fosho, this is about my sister and me. She's trying to expand off what she got and wants me to run this part," I lied, hoping that this shit didn't backfire. Premium lifted his brow as if I was fucking with him.

"Kali, wants to dabble in drugs when she's making a killing off of sheets? You got to be playing." He laughed. I shook my head and rubbed my beard.

"Nah, I'm dead ass. So just give us a price," I demanded. I could see the wheels spinning in his head.

"Twenty-five a key," he said.

"Cool, I'll take ten. Give me to the end of the week to get your money," I agreed. Premium stood up and held his hand out. I stood up and shook his hand, sealing the deal.

KALI

"I'm so glad you let me off tonight. My mind ain't been on work today at all." Myia sighed.

We were walking through Green Hills doing a little retail therapy and finding something for one of my worker's birthdays tonight. I could tell from Myia's voice that something was bothering her, but I didn't know if I wanted to ask because I knew it had something to do with my damn brother.

"Well, where's your mind been at because we can't have no slip-ups when it comes to my money?" I asked. I didn't mean to come off as harsh, but hell, we cannot bring emotions into the workplace.

"You know one thing about me ain't nothing about to mess up my flow of money. But, you know I shut down early last night and went home. How come when I got home Kalicio wasn't there," she said as we walked into the Louis Vuitton store.

"Myia, where was he then?" I asked. She stopped walking and picked up a bag off the shelf, and then she looked up at me.

"With another bitch. He thinks I don't know shit, but I know what I need to know. I was waiting on that ass when he came in the house last night," she said.

I wanted to bust out laughing because I can see Myia and my brother going at it. Sometimes I think Kalicio is scared of Myia's ass.

"What he say?" I asked dying to know.

"He ain't say a motherfucking thing. I did all the talking. I told him to wrap whatever he had going on with the bitch otherwise the shit ain't gone be cute!" she spat. I shook my head.

Myia was a good girl and loyal as fuck. I couldn't see how he could do something like that to her. That shit was between them though. I wasn't getting in it.

"See that's why I ain't got time to get my feelings caught up in no man because I know I would end up in jail," I admitted.

"Don't you want a family one day, KK? This life is ok, but shit, it's got to get lonely at the top?" Myia said.

I thought about what she said, and yeah, I've thought about kids and even marriage, but right now, my plate was full.

"Whatever happens happens. Meanwhile, I want this bag right here," I said quickly changing the conversation and heading to the counter to purchase the bag that I had grabbed.

Myia and I finished up at the mall and decided to grab a bite to eat before parting ways. Myia and I stopped at The Cheesecake Factory since we were right next door. We were sitting at the table sipping on our drinks when I saw Myia's eyes start to wonder.

"What the hell you looking at? Do I need to get my guys in here?" I asked. Baby trust, wherever I went, my security wasn't far. You may think you didn't see them, but they were close.

"Girl no, dude right at this table over your shoulder on the left. Synzari motherfucking Menace. He was so fine in school, and he still is," she whispered.

"Wait, that's his name for real?" I asked. She nodded her head.

"Synzari Menace. Last I heard he was working under Premium. I don't know," she said.

I had to see this guy, so I casually turned around and looked over my shoulder. He was so fine that I almost choked on my damn drink,. He was my complexion, but I couldn't tell if he was mixed with something or not. The bronze color of his yellow skin was covered in tattoos. His hair was in two French braids on his head. His beard was long and fit his face perfectly. Child, when he licked his lips, and we locked eyes, I quickly turned away.

"Bitch, now he's looking over here," Myia whispered, playing it off. I giggled and took a sip of my drink. Myia kicked me underneath the table.

"Ladies, don't I know you?" a deep voice sent chills down my spine. Myia smirked, and she responded.

"I went to school with you," I peeped his attire and looked at him up and down. He looked like he had a little bit of money.

"I'm Synzari," he said holding his hand out for me to shake.

"Kali," I answered. Bitch, I was trying to hold my composure, but this man was making my coochie twerk.

"I just felt the need to come and speak because I saw that we were making googly eyes with one another." He laughed which caused me to laugh also.

"Googly eyes, really? I mean you aite," I lied. The waiter walked over with our food, which was good because I was starving.

"Well, I'll let you ladies enjoy your food," he said.

"Yeah, don't want to keep your girlfriend waiting," I threw out there. I peeped the girl sitting at the booth with him.

"My girlfriend doesn't even know she's my girlfriend yet," he said as he winked his eye. I turned around, and Myia was staring at me all crazy.

"What?" I asked. She shook her head.

"I see some pretty mixed yellow babies in the near future." She giggled. Myia was too much, and I wasn't trying to hear shit she was talking.

Myia

COMING from nothing Kalicio and his sister was all I had here in Nashville. I came here from Memphis, TN as a runaway when I was seventeen. Once I made it to Nashville, it was new territory and survival of the fittest. My first week here I was able to get on at Popeyes Chicken. I lived in and out of hotels for about a month. The money was ok, but I needed more. I was trying to get a place, but I knew nobody at the time. Then I started stripping once I turned eighteen. Once that cash flow came in, one of the girls I worked with helped me get my own place.

One night my life changed forever when Kalicio stepped foot in the club with his sister. I was scared as hell to go to their booth. I don't know if I looked lost or in trouble, but Kalicio swept me off my feet. He was the same age as me, but I could tell it was some money being made. Kali reached out to me asking me about my family, and I told her my story. Since then she's been like a big sister/mother figure for both Kalicio and I. I owed them my life, and that's why I was so hurt to find out that Kalicio was even stepping out on me. He knew that I was about that life and I feared no bitch, so I don't know why he wanted to see that side of me. I just know that whatever he had going on with this July bitch had better be dead. I didn't understand why he wanted to be under Premium any fucking way. Being greedy was what he was doing, and I pray that it doesn't come back on his ass.

After Kali and I finished our food, we went our separate ways and planned to link later when it came time to go out. I needed this little break from work because I knew that tomorrow it was back to the basics with new orders.

SYNZARI

"How you just gone leave from the table and go talk to some other bitches, Syn? You just rude as hell!" Ava spat.

This was why I was single; at least I thought I was last I checked. These hoes get an ounce of niceness, and they swear we in a damn relationship. I pulled the money out of my pocket and threw it on the table because I was trying to remain calm.

"Look, first off, I was single as hell last time I checked. A nigga tried to be nice and feed your hungry ass but you up here worried about somebody else, not that I got to explain myself. Wait, I don't have to explain myself, so this conversation is fucking over. That's for the ticket, and you can catch an Uber home," I said getting up from the table.

"You ain't shit, nigga!" she yelled.

The patrons of the restaurant were looking and shit. I keep strolling on up out that piece. When I got in the car, I lit my damn blunt and sat there taking it to the head. My mind drifted off to something that I needed to take care of tonight before this damn party. When you heard my name, Synzari Menace or just Syn, you knew it wasn't nothing nice. I was a certified shooter. I didn't mind getting my hands dirty for the right price. I slept peacefully every night, but I was a legit menace in these streets. Premium kept me on his payroll, but I also did my own shit. I was cold in the game and never got caught slipping. They way I moved was calculated. I got close to all my hits. That way they wouldn't know who did what. I still was cool with motherfuckers that I had killed people they knew, but they never knew it was me. They would confide in me and all that.

I was low in everything I did. Nobody knew where I laid my head. Every female that I came in contact with we went to the fucking hotel. I can't let no hoe knowing my moves, and when they got mad, it was a problem. I was the only child. My mother was still alive and living her life because I made sure she didn't want for anything. She and her little friends stayed on the go taking trips. She was my love, and she deserved it. I didn't have no woman and no kids besides my granny, Gran Mae to splurge on. All that shit went out the window when I saw Kali's fine ass today. I spotted her and Myia when they walked into the restaurant. Kali was so bossed up that she was up there with a lot of heavyweights in the game here in the city. When I first heard of her, I thought she was in the drug game, but she was into that money making shit. With counterfeiting, she took certain risks that a lot of motherfuckers wouldn't dare take due to the time behind it.

One thing for sure that shit was a huge turn on. I was gone pull her little hard ass. I needed her on my arm. I finished the blunt and placed the roach in the ashtray. There was a knock on the window. I shook my head because this bitch had to be crazy.

"Get the fuck off my car before I shoot yo ass!" I yelled.

She was yelling, and spit was flying all on the window. I put my shit in reverse and backed the fuck out. See, I didn't have time for this type of shit. I hit the interstate. It was time for me to go handle this wax.

Later That Night

Kali

. . .

I WAS ready to fucking turn-up tonight. It had been a minute since these folks seen Kali on the scene. I stood in the floor length mirror taking in my outfit. Rocking a silk ruffle Dolce & Gabbana shirt with a Dolce & Gabbana duchess skirt, this outfit was everything, and you know I had to step out in the Dolce & Gabbana peep toe lace-up boots that wasn't even fully out yet. My long hair was curled in wands curls with a part down the middle. After I finished applying some gloss, I threw my shades on and headed to scoop Myia.

The ride to Myia's was a turnt one. I had been pre-gaming a little bit before I left the house, so I had a slight buzz. I wasn't going to let anything mess up this night for me. I whipped into my brother's driveway, and I didn't see his truck. I pulled out my phone and shot Myia a text letting her know that I was outside. I tapped the steering wheel to the beat of the music. Myia came strutting out to the car, and I did a little jig because baby she didn't half step with her assemble tonight. Myia hopped in the car.

"Ok bitch, I see you!" I yelled. Myia did a little twerk in her seat.

"Girl, hurry up and get me to the club because a drink is needed, and I'm ready to shake my ass," Myia said.

When we pulled up at the spot, the parking lot was packed so I could only imagine how it looked on the inside. I pulled straight up to the front, and one of my security took my whip while Myia and I made our way to the entrance. We didn't stand in lines, and I wasn't about to start now. The niggas were drooling, and the females were whispering. When I stepped up to the door, one of the huge guards gave me the once-over.

"Kali, what's up? Aw shit, the boss done stepped out. Your brother up in there," he said.

I knew my brother probably would show, so it didn't bother me. He let us in the club, and we made our way inside. The crowd was thick, and I wasn't one to mingle around in it. I headed straight to our section.

Kalicio

. . .

I HAD rode out with Premium and his nigga Syn to come to the club. I was trying my best to get on this nigga's good side and stay there. Here I was chilling in the section kicking shit and throwing back shots when Myia and my sister walk in. I had to keep Kali's ass away from Premium because I knew my shit would get blown if he started speaking to Kali about her getting in the business.

"Hey, baby." I broke my gaze and looked up at July. She was smiling from ear to ear.

"Aw wassup," I said looking around her to see where KK and Myia were walking.

I watched them as they walked to a section that was across from us. The way it was set up I could see them clearly, but they really couldn't see over in our section. July turned around, and her eyes went to where I was looking.

"I see your sister in here, and ain't that your little girlfriend?" she asked.

At this point, I didn't give a shit about her brother seeing or hearing this, but I was about to check her ass. I grabbed her arm pulling her down towards me.

"That's right, my woman is in here, and if you start some shit, that's your ass. It's a wrap. Know your place!" I spat, letting her arm go. Premium wasn't shit. He took a sip out of his glass.

"You heard the man," was all he said. July looked shocked hell I knew I was. July rolled her eyes and walked out of the section.

"Sorry about that man," I apologized to him.

"Man, that shit is between y'all, but why your sister ain't come over here and speak?" he asked. See, I knew once he spotted her he would question it, and I had to think fast.

"You know Kali is discreet as shit. She doesn't even want nobody to know her new move. She sends her best wishes though," I told him. I knew what I was about to do would be pushing, but I pulled my phone out and sent Myia a text.

Me: Send a bottle to Premium's booth. I got you when we get home.

Wifey: Whatever, nigga. Let me see that bitch back over there, and I'm going in both y'all shit.

Me: Gal, don't start, I got the deal

Wifey: I guess.

I shoved my phone back in my pocket. She thought she had an attitude now, just wait until I ask her this big favor I needed to ask her.

MYIA

*A*s soon as we walked in the club and got settled in our section, I spotted Kalicio's big teddy bear looking ass and July all in his face. I knew KK could feel the steam that radiated off my back. She was in her own world and on her fourth drink. If I didn't know any better, I'd say she was scoping out Synzari. Then this nigga had his nerve to text me asking me to send a bottle. At this moment, I couldn't stand Kalicio, but at the same time, I wasn't going to mess up what he was trying to do. I knew that he hated working under KK because he couldn't stand being ordered by a woman, and even though she was older, he felt he needed the lead in something. So, he was doing all that he could to get plugged in with Premium. Motioning for the waitress to make her way back over, I spotted July eye-fucking me in the crowd. I giggled because this wasn't what she wanted. Needing to take my eye off her for just a second, I placed this order.

"Can you send a bottle of D'usse over to that booth please," I ordered and shoved the girl a few bills. KK nudged me.

"Why the fuck this chick keeps looking over here, you know her?" she asked. We both watched as she made her way over to Premium's booth.

"That's your brother's little hoe. I feel I'm gone have to show my ass tonight," I admitted.

One thing about KK, she was a classy bitch, and you wouldn't see her out in public fighting, but baby, I was the opposite. We watched as the bottle girl took over the bottle that I sent, and July settled right beside him on the couch.

"Myia, it may not be all that you think, but the way these drinks got me feeling bitch, if you jump, then I'm jumping too." She shrugged, which made me do a double take and look her way.

I threw the rest of my drink back and placed the glass on the table. Lil Baby & Gunna's "Drip Too Hard" came blaring through the speakers. KK stood up; this was her shit too. Bobbing my head, I did my little two-step beside her but kept my eye on my man across from me. The entire song you can call me what you want but this hoe was trying to get a reaction out of me. She was throwing her ass all in Kalicio's face and what bothered me was that he was allowing this shit. I couldn't take no more. I stormed out of VIP and made my way across the floor not even telling KK I'd be back. Premium was that nigga, so he had his entourage with him and security was beefed up.

"Excuse me," security stopped me and placed his hand to my chest. I looked down at his hand.

"We need to get in there with my brother," KK's voice came from behind me. I turned around. I didn't even know she followed me.

"Kali, you know I'm on the job, and I can't just let you in like that," security told KK. She knew every damn body.

"We are guests, and I just sent a bottle over here," I jumped in.

"What seems to be the problem?" another voice came from behind me.

Synzari was making his way through the crowd. Aw yeah, I knew we were about to get in now. He smiled when he saw KK, and she was blushing her ass off too.

"They good, big dog," he said not even knowing we were about to come up in here and wreak havoc.

The security moved out of the way and let us in. Synzari was busy in KK face, so I made my way over to Kalicio who was busy getting a lap dance from July. Premium saw me coming, and you should've seen his face. He tried to signal Kalicio that I was making my way over there. Before he looked my way, I had grabbed a beer bottle from the table and cracked that bitch open on the table. I stood there with this broken bottle, and my brow lifted because he knew what the fuck was going on,

"Damn baby, wassup?" he stuttered.

"What the fuck I tell you?" I spat. All the niggas were doing their ooh and ahhs egging shit on.

"You want to keep playing with me about this low budget ass bitch. Motherfucker, you knew I was in this club, and you in here parading this bitch around like my motherfucking name ain't Myia Spence. I know you fucking lying!" I yelled. Kalicio knew once I snapped that it would be hard to calm me down.

"Ooh this just too much for me," July had the nerve to say. She tried to walk by me, and with my left hand, I grabbed that hoe by her neck and had my right hand pressing this bottle up under her chin.

"You thot ass bottom of the barrel ass bitch. I can't stand hoes like you. You big and bad and want to mess with another woman's man out in the open then you need to be ready for the consequences, bitch. I will cut your ass in so many pieces and serve you at my Fourth of July barbeque. Play with it, hoe!" I said through gritted teeth.

"Ok, that's enough. We can't get blood on these designer digs boo," KK said, reaching for the bottle out of my hand.

At that moment, I felt like my love for Kalicio was diminishing. During all of this, he sat there and didn't say shit. It's funny the things people would do to sell their soul. I was hurt as hell, but I wasn't about to let that show. KK was drunk I could tell. She went over to her brother.

"You ain't shit for that. I hope Myia leaves your ass!" she spat. KK walked off with Synzari on her heels, and I turned to Kalicio.

"Get your motherfucking ass home now!" I yelled.

Kalicio was far from a bitch he would speak me out and jack me up in a heartbeat, but he would never put his hands on me in any other way. I think he knew how much he fucked up which had his head fucked up.

Synzari

The moment I saw Kali again, a nigga was excited as hell. They looked like they were trying to get in Premium section, which they were, but I didn't know shit was going to pop off like that otherwise I wouldn't have let them in. I done been around some rugged thugged out chicks before, but I wasn't expecting her homegirl to crack open no beer bottle like that. What stunned me was Premium didn't even try to stop the shit. That nigga didn't give a fuck about nobody, not even his own damn blood. I'm glad Kali interfered when she did. I wanted to exchange numbers with Kali because I wanted to get to know her on a more personal level.

We made it outside while she waited on her security to bring her car around. I took her in from head to toe, and she most definitely was somebody that I could see on my arms. She was bad, and she knew it.

"Why are you looking at me like I'm a piece of meat?" she asked with a slight smile. When I got nervous, I always toyed with my beard, so I started doing that out of habit.

"I'm debating if I should shoot my shot or not." I laughed. She glanced over her shoulder while her car pulled up.

"Well, I'm not going to be here all night, so you don't have much time to debate," she said basically telling me to shoot it.

"Is it ok if I have your number? I know you a busy woman," I asked.

She did this thing where she bit down on her lip as if she was thinking and reached for my phone. I watched as she placed her number in my phone and handed it back to me. She gave a wink and strutted to her car. Looking down at my phone, I smiled at the thought of getting to know her.

SYNZARI

Synzari Latrell Menace was my birth given name. At twenty-seven years old, I had made quite a life for myself. I wasn't out here in the streets flocking from hoe to hoe, I did my job well, and I stayed low key. My father was a cold-blooded killer, and he raised me to do the same. You know how when you grow up you have a different outlook on how you want your life to go then here comes somebody placing things on it, and it's either their way or no way. That was the kind of relationship I had with my father growing up. My father was so skilled at what he did that he could do it in his sleep. Me, on the other hand, I didn't want no parts, but it was forced on me.

I thought I wanted to take the easy route by selling drugs and getting fast cash, but I soon discovered hell I wasn't about that life either. My father always told me let a man fear what he doesn't know and forever move that way. Being in the drug business caused me to interact with a lot of people, so everyone had their minds set on what you did. They think they knew how you moved and how to operate because you were in the open and vulnerable to others. Being a killer, nobody knew just how I got down except those that paid me a pretty penny. They never knew how I operated, so a lot feared me because I was quiet and observant. I could sit in the room with a hundred niggas, and I would be the one feared because nothing got a reaction out of me. Motherfuckers would ask why this nigga even here? Truthfully, I knew they ain't want to ever know what I did on the receiving end.

Later on, that night when I got home, I laid in bed going back and forth on whether I should hit the send button. I didn't want to come off as an irking ass nigga, but I did want to know if Kali made it home safely. As I started to twirl the hairs on my beard, I said fuck it and pressed send. Laying the phone on my chest, my work phone started buzzing. I hopped up fast as hell because I knew when that line went off, it was critical. I read the text that gave me details on what I needed to do. After storing it in my memory, I deleted the text and got dressed. I heard my other phone going off, but I didn't have time to even check it, and I bet it was Kali hitting me back. When money calls nothing else matters.

Kalicio

MYIA HAD me so fucked up for showing her ass in the club. I was doing about eighty all the way home. Yeah, I left when she told me, but don't get shit confused because I run shit. Myia was just in her feelings right now, and she needed to understand what the hell I had going on. When I walked in the house, I looked around, and I could tell she hadn't made it here yet, which was cool because that gave me time to register everything that just happened. Then my mind went to KK, my own damn sister. I had some words for her ass too. Looking around at the home that Myia and I had created together just pissed me off.

I heard the door beep, and Myia came storming in. I can tell she had been crying because her makeup had been smeared. She flung her purse on the couch. I stood there with my arms crossed and a look on my face that let her know that I meant business and don't start no shit.

WOP! WOP!

Myia had thrown two punches at me. Before I knew what the hell happened, she was about to throw another, but I caught her arm mid-swing.

"Chill the fuck out!" I spat. Myia jerked away from me. She was breathing like a raging bull.

"You want me to chill the fuck out when I should be packing my shit and leaving. Matter of fact that sounds like a great idea. You embarrassed me tonight. I have never felt so disrespected in my life. I told you to dead that shit with ole girl, did I not?" she yelled.

Rubbing my hands over my face, I let out a huge sigh.

"Look, I told her ass that she needed to know her place because you were in there. She did that shit to get a reaction out of you, and you fell right into her trap!" I roared. Fuck! That didn't sound good. Myia came charging at me again.

"You bout a dumb motherfucker, did you just hear the shit that you just said. You told her to know her place, but meanwhile, you let her do whatever the hell she wanted to do when you knew I was sitting across from her. If you can't control your hoes, then why do you have them? Did I not ask you to dead it the other night once you got this deal? Therefore, it should've been dealt with. There was no way I should've walked in there and seen that shit. On top of that, you just sat there like wasn't shit going to happen. You lucky KK came and got that shit out of my hand because July was going to be every month of the year once I got done slicing and dicing her ass. I can't fucking believe you, Kalicio," she cried and marched off.

There was no way I could let this shit go down like this. I followed Myia to the bedroom.

"Look, Myia. I swear I'm sorry. A nigga's been drinking." She held her hand up in my face shutting me up.

"Why is that the first thing a man says when he gets caught? Kalicio, I really think you didn't give a damn about tonight. Because one you knew that we were all coming out tonight for Mercy's birthday. You always want to try me then when I go off you try to make me feel like I'm in the wrong. Let that had of been me and boy you would've shown your big overgrown ass in that club. I hope you know that it's a wrap. If I find out you still affiliated with her in any shape or fashion, I'm leaving your ass," she hissed.

I sucked my teeth because I knew Myia ass wasn't going nowhere. I took a seat on the side of the bed.

"You work tomorrow?" I asked Myia. I needed to set my other plan in motion.

"Yes, why you want to know?" she said rudely. Her attitude was pissing me off.

"Premium paid me for sheets tonight, but it's a rushed order, so he needs them ASAP. He paid for 250 stacks," I told her. Myia shook her head.

"Kalicio, you know that it already takes a damn week to make sheets and that shit can't be rushed because it's a process. Anything not done right that shit will show up as counterfeit and that's our ass," she replied.

One thing about Myia was she ain't play about her job. She was loyal as hell to Kali that's why I would never tell her what I had going on, and she was supposed to be my ride or die.

"It won't be our ass because he's already aware of that. Look, just do the sheets and get at me when they done," I demanded.

First thing in the morning I was heading over to Kali and get in her shit.

KALI

The knocking on my bedroom door pissed me off waking me up out of my sleep. Looking over at the clock, I realized that I had slept longer than I needed to. I really needed to go to the warehouse and check up on things. The knocking returned, so I kicked the covers off my legs and eased out of bed.

"What is it?" I groaned, opening the door. Marisol stood there holding me a glass of her special Bloody Mary that she made when she knew I had a long night.

"Gracias," I sighed.

"Tu hermano esta abajo," Marisol spoke, and I didn't have the time for no translation.

"English, Marisol," I sighed in irritation.

"Your brother is downstairs." She nodded.

"Thank you, tell him I'll be down when I get good and ready," I told her closing my bedroom door.

I didn't know what the hell he thought this was popping up over here like he was about to put me in my place. I knew exactly why he was here. Opening the door, I walked out on my bedroom patio and looked out at the water. Sipping from the Bloody Mary gave me some immediate relief.

"You got me fucked up sending Marisol to say that shit like I'm one of your workers!" Kalicio spat.

I turned around looking at his big ass. Rolling my eyes, I turned back around and continue to stare at the water.

"Last I checked you were a worker, baby brother." I laughed. If I knew anything, I knew my brother and how to crush his big boy ego.

"That shit you said last night was foul, KK. You supposed to be my motherfucking blood, my sister!" he yelled. Now you see why I tried my best to stay the hell out of their relationship.

"First of all, you not about to barge in my house and tell me I'm wrong for what the fuck I said. Blood or not your ass was wrong. You a stupid motherfucker and you only think about yourself and how it benefits you. You sat up there and disrespected your woman and for what? You brought that shit to your doorstep. I could care less about your outside dealings or whatever it is that you trying to get off the ground. But when that shit clouds the judgment of one of my most important workers to where I have to question can she do her job, and it's put my shit at stake, then baby brother we have a problem!" I yelled, standing toe to toe with Kalicio. I could smell the mint from his breath because all he was doing was blowing off steam.

"You still were foul," was all he could say.

"No, what's foul is this stench of an aura that I'm getting from you. I can't put my finger on it, but I'm getting some bad vibes from you. Please dismiss yourself from my house," I said turning back around to finish my drink.

I loved my brother with all my heart, but something wasn't right with him. Walking back into the room, I placed my drink on the dresser and pulled out my phone. Synzari had already scored a strike in my book. How the hell he texted me last night but didn't respond to my text? This is why I didn't have time for the dealings that came along with dating a man.

Myia

. . .

My mind was all over the place, and I was slick ready to go home. I hate that this shit had my mental fucked up. I watched as the workers were handling the printed sheets for Kalicio. I had to get this shit done while Canton ass wasn't here. If he knew what was going on, he would tell KK so fast. I don't know where Premium thought he was going to pass this money off at, but with this rushed ass job this entire batch was traceable. If this got in the wrong hands, this could come back on Kali, and this would be all bad.

"What you looking at?" I yelled at Chris.

"Nothing, are we getting paid for this batch because this shit here I really don't want no parts of if Ms. Kusain ain't signed off on it? A nigga is already in the hot seat," he had the nerve to say.

This was the very reason we had the right workers in this business because we were loyal to one another. Kalicio came dragging his heavy foot ass in the room. I looked back at the Chris.

"If anything goes wrong Kalicio is taking the fall for everybody. This is his order." I said, and I didn't even care. Kalicio stood there with a look of disdain on his face. I walked passed him, and he grabbed my arm.

"You still on that fuck shit?" he asked. All I could do was laugh.

"Fuck shit, really Kalicio? You must want to feel these hands again. How about you get your money and get the hell out of here, so we can get started on the real shit that we're already behind on. I hope all that you're doing is worth losing your woman over," I told him.

"Oh, so now you leaving me after last night?" he asked.

"This is bigger than last night," I said. I was so disappointed in him, and he just couldn't see it. He did what he did best, which was sucked his teeth and left.

"Go ahead and get things going on our original order," I told Chris as I headed to the office.

I hope his ass was long gone so I took my time walking through the warehouse. Most of the crew was here, and they had a dice game going on. If KK walked in here and seen that shit, she would go off. They knew to move out the way of the cameras too with their slick asses.

I pressed the code on the door and locked it behind me once I stepped in. Walking over to the bar, I grabbed a glass and poured me a shot of Tequila. It was much needed as its smooth taste went down my throat. Plopping down in the chair, I rubbed my temples and tried to absorb and break down all the things that had transpired. I needed to get my shit together and fast because ain't no way a nigga was about to have me off my game.

SYNZARI

*C*oming back from Arkansas, a nigga was tired. Having to leave town like that was the norm for me when it came time for a job that needed to be handled. Not being able to talk to Kali, I just hope that she wasn't pissed. My focus had solely been on completing my mission and getting back to Nashville. I sat in the driveway and stared at the front of the house that I always came to upon completing dirty work. It was my peace and no matter the mood I'm in coming here, was like a recharge.

My father's mother, Gran Mae would bend over backwards for me as I was coming up. The funniest thing was the way her and my mother competed for my love. They just didn't know I loved both of them equally. Gran Mae was just more stationary than my mother was. My father despised our relationship because theirs were strained. Gran Mae knew exactly what my father did, and she didn't like it one bit. It would kill her if she knew that I followed in his footsteps. Gran Mae thought I was a truck driver, which required long trips on the road.

Slowly opening up the door, I eased out of the car. Pulling my hoodie over my head, I looked around and headed towards the porch. My grandmother refused to move out of North Nashville. She still lived in a somewhat bad part, but of course, most of the older houses were being torn down and rebuilt. A company wanted to pay top dollar to get my grandmother's property, and I turned around and paid them just to renovate so that her old house wouldn't be an eyesore in the neighborhood. Granny wasn't going anywhere long as I had breath in my body.

Using my key, I entered the house, and the homely feeling immediately put me at ease. The smell of something baking and Gain laundry detergent put a smile on my face. I headed towards the kitchen and peeped around the corner. Granny was sitting there at the kitchen table watching her court shows on the flat screen TV that was hung on the wall. Granny had to have a TV in the kitchen; she demanded that.

"Latrell, don't be creeping up on me boy, you gone catch some heat," she said aloud not even taking her eyes off the TV. She had a nigga on the spot, and I couldn't do nothing but laugh. Granny hated my first name because it had sin in it even though it was spelled differently. She most definitely hated my last name Menace, so she called me by my middle name Latrell. Shaking my head, I walked into the kitchen and placed a kiss on her soft cheek.

"Granny, how you even know it was me?" I asked.

Granny was beautiful. She didn't even look like she was seventy-six years old. One thing about granny was she didn't play about her health. She was active as hell and looked good for her age.

"Latrell, you the only one with a key unless it was your father returning from the gates of hell!" she spat.

I laughed and took a seat beside her and started grabbing some clothes from the basket of laundry she was folding.

"You ain't got no filter, granny." I laughed.

"What the hell I need a filter for? I ain't ever been the type to add sugar to shit. So, where you coming from this time?" she asked. That guilt hit a nigga right in the stomach.

"Arkansas, a nigga is tired too. I just want to eat and cuddle up with my granny. I ain't trying to watch this shit though," I said pointing to the TV.

"Watch your damn mouth, before I knock that beard clean off your face. I cooked yesterday, so it's some leftovers in the fridge, and I got some cobbler in the oven. Talking about you don't want to watch this shit. Boy, you learn something from these court shows. Have you talked to your mama?" she asked.

"I talked to her last week. She was in Cabo," I answered. Hopping up, I made my way to the fridge so that I could feed my face. After fixing a plate, I placed it in the microwave and sat back down beside Gran Mae. Pulling out my phone, I scrolled down to Kali's number because I wanted to shoot her a text. I just sat there going back and forth with myself. Finally, I gave in and sent her a text hoping that she replied.

Me: Hey just got back in town, had an emergency.

After I hit send, I placed the phone on the table and removed my food from the microwave. I bowed my head and blessed my food before I dug in.

"So when you gone bring me some grandbabies?" my granny asked. This was the one question that she never stopped asking.

"When I find the right one. I'm not about to reproduce with just anybody just because you want a grandbaby," I told her.

"Well shit, I hope it's before I croak over." She laughed. Shaking my head, I filled my mouth with some food. My phone buzzed, and I grabbed it so fast.

Kali: I guess I don't have time for the bullshit, sir.
Me: I wouldn't bullshit you. I'm dead ass.
Kali: I may have some time for you later.
Me: Hmu if you do
Kali: Yeah. Ok.

A nigga was grinning hard. I could tell Kali was going to be a hard pleaser. My phone buzzed again, and I picked it up, and it was a text from Premium

Prem: Spot in 30.
Me: Aite.

I wasn't thrilled that I had to leave back out because I liked to chill when I came back in town, but after whatever this was, I was going to come back here. Finishing up my plate, I washed my dish and cleaned up my mess.

"I got to make a run right quick. I'll be back in a little bit. You need anything?" I asked.

"Grab me twenty in Jumbo Bucks," she told me. Her little gambling ass.

"Aite," I told her as I planted a kiss on her forehead.

KALICIO

It was time for the exchange, and I wasn't the least bit nervous. I had gotten comfortable with Premium, so this exchange might be easier than I planned. I reached for the bag I had on the passenger side and placed it in my lap. Opening the bag, I thumbed through the money. I had placed real bills on top of all the money in case he was to inspect it. Satisfied I zipped the bag up and got out the car. Walking into the meeting spot, I was greeted by his crew. I dapped up everyone. Some I was familiar with from the club.

"What it do, homie?" I said dapping Premium up.

"Not shit. I'm not trying to be here all night," he said, making it even better for me. The quicker this transaction could happen, I could be on my way.

"Understandable, well here you go. It's all there," I told him handing him the bag.

This was the moment of truth, and I had to keep it cool. Premium unzipped the bag and looked inside. He pulled two stacks from the bag and thumb through the money like I knew he would.

"I don't have to sit here and count this, do I?" he asked. *You be a fool not to.* I thought.

"I got all night. It's on you," I told him. Don't get me wrong the money was all there. The money was even passable until somebody marked that shit. Premium nodded to one of his little goons. The guy stepped forward and handed me another bag. Opening the bag, I looked inside and was satisfied with the product.

"May I?" I asked. I wanted to test the product making sure it was what I wanted. Ain't that some shit, yeah, I know. I reached and grabbed a small pocketknife opening up I poked one of the bags and dipped my finger inside. I rubbed my finger across my gums, and that shit was pure and on point.

"So, we good?" I asked. Premium held his hand out for me to shake.

"Tell Kali I wish y'all the best on this venture, and I'm glad she came to me instead of going to some sucker ass nigga," he said. Shit, I forgot that damn quick that I had put Kali name in this shit.

"Will do, take care," I told him and hauled ass up out that place.

My first stop was straight to the trap house I had so I could set up with my crew that I had formed to get this shit packaged up and on the streets, asap.

The adrenaline that pumped through my veins was so powerful that you would've thought I was on some type of medicine. This shit really worked. I made it to North Nashville in no time. I pulled up at one of the spots we were going to use. This white cat name Carlton let me use his basement, the perfect setup for the new nosey white neighbors that lived in the neighborhood. Once the product was bagged up, his girlfriend would pack it up and drop it off for distribution.

Carlton was one of them motherfuckers that worked with some high-class people, white collar shit, but he didn't mind powdering his nose. So long as he was getting his nose candy he was all down for us using his basement to cook up.

I walked around the basement watching my workers work, I trusted my team, but motherfuckers still needed watching. The words exchanged with my sister earlier played over and over in my head. Some would think I was wrong for doing what I did, but unless you had to work under her, you couldn't see how I was treated. KK was stubborn as hell, so I knew we wouldn't speak for a minute because that's just how she was when she was mad. Now that she and Myia done clicked up, I was just going to have to keep my distance.

Synzari

When I pulled up at the spot to meet Premium, this nigga was wired and amped to go to the strip club. I wasn't big on strip clubs, but I assume it was business. I was only going to stay for a minute and take my ass back to my granny house.

"Bout time your ass showed up!" Premium yelled. We exchanged daps and took a seat.

"Wassup, you got a job for me?" I inquired.

"Nah, I really needed you here when Kalicio came through with his drop just in case that nigga jumped stupid, but shit went smoothly. So, we about to head out and spend some money on these strippers," Premium laughed.

"I was really trying to chill, but I guess I can come out for a little," I told him.

Premium was on that flashy shit tonight, so I knew what this was. This nigga wasn't lowkey about nothing he did. Premium and his crew dispersed to their cars, and I hopped in my truck. I wasn't riding with nobody cause when it came time for me to go, I was vamping like a thief in the night.

We pulled up at Tootie B's a well-known strip joint that would always let us come in and take over and basically have no regards to the rules of the place. I made sure I had my heat on me just in case a nigga got out of character. Stepping out the car, I made my way inside and found me a nice spot in the booth we had and got comfortable. Premium had ordered a shit load of bottles, and the strippers were flocking to our section like flies on shit. I enjoyed a Corona since I wasn't in the mood for no drink. The DJ came over the speakers.

"Y'all ready for The Black Out?" he asked. The patrons of the place yelled out.

Now, what the hell was the black out? The lights went out, and all these damn UV and neon lights came on. The dancers were in glow in the dark attire some had body paint on them that only covered important parts. This shit was crazy. I touched my hip because if I had to come out blasting, then I wasn't sparing a soul. This was the perfect set up for a nigga to try his hand. It gets dark, and motherfuckers want to creep.

"Here nigga, enjoy yourself and stop sitting there like a married ass man!" Premium yelled over the loud music. He handed me a stack while one chick was grinding on him so hard she'd probably come up with a rash, and the other had her ass all in his face while he palmed it.

Grabbing the bills that he gave me, I laid them in my lap. This nigga really in here handing out stacks of hundred-dollar bills. This motherfucker is stupid as hell. This thick little something made her way over to me, and she had a look in her eyes like she ain't want to be here either. There was an innocence about her. She was wearing body paint, so a nigga could tell her body was banging.

"Can I dance for you?" she asked, even her voice depicted innocence. I gave her a head nod. She seductively moved her body, so I took another sip of my beer and let her do her.

"You act like you not interested?" she whispered, looking back at me. I let out a little laugh.

"I would much rather be at home. This is not my kind of party really. I could say the same thing about you though," I returned.

"This is my second night, and I honestly hate it, but I really need the money," she admitted. I could read body language like a motherfucker, and that was the vibe I was getting.

"Well, if it makes you comfortable, you can stay here of course until I decide to leave," I told her. She smiled and nodded her head and continued dancing.

Looking down at the money that sat in my lap, I removed the band that was holding it in place. Thumbing through the bills I was going to give her majority of it, but I wanted to count it first because a nigga was finna pocket some of it. I could barely see, but the black lights lit the money up. As I counted the money, something wasn't right. I held one of the bills closer to the light and saw the security strip, so I grabbed the other bill out the pile and held it to the light. This bill didn't have the same strip.

"Get up right quick," I voiced to the girl. She looked confused, but she got up.

I placed some more bills up to the light all, which didn't have a security strip like the first bill. Reaching into my pocket, I pulled out my own cash that I carried and thumbed to a hundred-dollar bill and held it up to the light. This bill had a security strip. Now I know I wasn't no fool, but if I'm not mistaken these other bills without a strip couldn't be legit. I smiled at the girl, so she wouldn't think nothing was wrong and handed her a couple hundred from my stack.

"I'm about to dip so you can take this for your trouble," I told her. She looked at the money.

"Thank you so much." She smiled placing the money in her titty and walking off. I leaned over towards Premium.

"We need to talk ASAP without ass in your face," I said in a serious tone.

I could tell he wasn't hearing it, but I gave him that look like I meant business. I stood up and made my way to the restroom. Once inside, I checked the stalls and made sure no one was inside. Premium walked in with a scowl on his face.

"What the fuck is up, I was trying to have a good time?" he asked.

"Nigga, where this money come from?" I asked, holding up the bills in his face.

"I made that drop with Kalicio tonight. That's the money he gave me, why?" he asked.

"Nigga this shit is as fake as the girl ass you had in your face. You ain't check that shit before he left knowing his background?" I asked. I could tell Premium was tight as hell.

"I thumbed through it," he said.

"Look at this shit. This is the money you gave me." I reached into my pocket and pulled out my own money. "This is my money. Come here," I told him walking out the bathroom back into the dark club.

I walked over to one of the lights and held both bills up to the light showing him how one contained a security strip, and the other didn't.

I switched out some more of his bills showing him how all these bitches were fake. His jaw was twitching, and I knew he was ready for some shit. This nigga had pulled a fast one on the wrong one.

"I'm going to handle this shit in the morning, call an emergency meeting because they done crossed the wrong motherfucker!" he spat.

PREMIUM

Now I was one of them people that didn't play when it came to my money or business. The fact that everyone knew that, and this nigga and his sister decide they wanted to play me. I was about to wreak havoc on this motherfucking city. When Syn left, I couldn't even focus on the strippers. My niggas could sense something was up in my change of demeanor.

"Man, leave all that shit and let's bounce," I told my homeboy. Them hoes would find out soon enough that all the money they received tonight was fake as shit. Fuck! That shit was going to come back to me.

Growing up, I was a spoiled ass rich kid simply because my father ran the drug business. I watched him like you would your favorite cartoon. I looked up to him and wanted to be just like him. The respect that he had from everyone here in the city was amazing, and I wanted that feeling. At first, when I took over my father's business people didn't think I had it in me to run the streets like my father did. So, it was show and prove on my end. Then people saw that I was ten times worse than my father was.

Kali ran her business just as bad as I ran mine, so for her to even cross me like this was fucking with me, but I was going to get to the bottom of it, and Synzari was going to help me.

* * *

THE NEXT MORNING, I stopped at Starbucks to grabbed me a caramel macchiato. Yeah, a nigga needed his dose of caffeine. I pulled up to the spot, grabbed my coffee, and hopped out the car. I pulled my hoodie over my head and fixed my Versace frames on my face.

"Waddup, Preme?" one of my guards spoke. I hit him with a head nod and walked in.

Everyone was here, and some even had sour looks on their faces because I called this meeting early as hell. I haven't even been asleep my damn self. I placed my coffee on the table and removed my hood looking at everyone.

"Sorry to get y'all out of bed early as hell and away from your families on this Sunday morning, but this shit is important. Another big organization has crossed us," I started talking.

"As y'all know I did a huge exchange with Kali and Kalicio Kusain yesterday. It was brought to my attention last night that they pulled a fast one on me, which I take the blame for not looking at the money, but if you know them you know that they run the biggest counterfeit ring. The bills that were exchanged for my product was fake as hell and this nigga out her pushing pure weight. Syn, I noticed you talking to Kali so continue with that shit, get closer than close. I want you to handle her and her brother. The rest of all y'all play with their team. I don't care if a motherfucker comes up missing every day until they get the picture!" I spat. By this time, I was steaming mad the thought of this shit pissed me off even more.

Everyone was speaking in their own conversations I guess shocked by what I had told them. Grabbing my coffee, I headed to my office to remove some money from the safe so that I could get Syn a deposit on his services. Syn followed, and I could tell something was bothering him.

"Wassup with you?" I asked.

"Man, I'm just thinking. Do you honestly think that Kali had anything to do with this for real? This shit was sloppy, and I feel that she doesn't move like that," he said. I knew what this was Syn was sniffing around Kali's ass and was feeling her.

"If this job is going to be hard for you then I can always find somebody else to do it. That's why I said get close. Research and do whatever you do before you kill someone!" I spat.

Kali

It was a new day, and I had time to refresh and get my mind back right. I had an order that needed to get out, so I was stopping by the warehouse to check and see the progress on it. When I got there, Myia was nowhere to be found. I wore flats today, so my steps couldn't be heard. I could hear laughs and shit talking in the distance. Once I rounded the corner, there was a full fledge dice game going on.

"What the fuck is this?" I yelled causing everyone to stop in their tracks and look up at me.

"Aw shit, KK, we were just passing the time until the sheets were ready," one of my workers said.

"Not on my fucking dime. Is this the shit y'all do? Maybe y'all ain't busy enough. Get this shit up before I dock your pay!" I yelled. They had me fucked up, and where the fuck was Myia? I took off upstairs to the office and walked in. Myia was sitting at the desk looking at the computer.

"Are you aware that there's a fucking dice game under your nose?" I asked her. She looked up and shook her head.

"No, I didn't, I was trying to finish up counting up this inventory," she said, letting out a sigh. Myia looked stressed. I placed my purse in the chair.

"Don't tell me you still fucked up about my dumb ass brother?" I asked.

"Girl, fuck him right now. We had words," she said. I laughed.

"Yeah we had words yesterday also, so he probably won't be speaking to me for a while," I admitted. Myia looked shocked.

"You don't have to take up for me, KK. I appreciate it, "she said.

"This ain't all about you, Myia. My business comes before anything," I told her.

I notice a shift in Miya's mood, and she wore a certain look on her face that look where you're fighting with something but holding it in. I wonder what that was all about.

My phone buzzed, and I glanced down at a text from Synzari.

Syn: Let me take you out.

Me: When?

Syn: Drop everything and let's just enjoy the day.

Me: I'm taking care of business right now, maybe later.

Syn: Ok, hmu.

I placed the phone down and glanced back up at Myia who had her head back in the computer.

"I'm about to make rounds on the floor," I told her.

When I came back downstairs, the little dice crew had cleaned up and were back at work like ain't shit happened. I made my way over to the eye of my work. I loved to watch everyone move in precision. You would think these folks had doctorates in making counterfeit money. I smiled and moved to the printer machines. Looking down I noticed a crumpled-up sheet of paper under the machine, so I reached down and picked it up. Unraveling the paper, it was a sheet, a not so good sheet.

"What is this?" I asked. The worker shrugged her shoulders, and I took the paper back upstairs to Myia.

"Y'all messing up on sheets now? When did this start happening?" I questioned, busting into the room.

"Um, I think that was a trial run your brother called in," she said. This motherfucker, I swear he was going to make me hurt him.

"Aite," was all I said.

Kalicio was moving fishy, and I knew it. I just couldn't put my finger on that shit. I folded the paper and placed it in my purse. There was a beating coming from the office door. Myia rushed over to the door and opened it.

"The hell going on?" she spat. One of my female workers had a tear-stained face.

"It's MJ. They found him dead," she cried. MJ was one of my OGs.

"Who the fuck will kill MJ, he ain't bother nobody?" I quizzed.

"Something ain't right, KK. They said he had a bill stuck in his chest a knife was holding it in place." She continued to cry. The details she was giving me was fucked up.

I rubbed my temples and tried to process this shit. I texted my security and let them know to look into this shit. If I didn't know nothing, I knew somebody was sending me a message, but why?

SYNZARI

I sat on the couch with my granny watching some movie she had found. She was pissed that I didn't come right back with her scratch-offs, so I was making it up to her by tormenting myself with one of her old movies. My mind wasn't even here it was on the task at hand, and it was a task that I didn't want to complete. I had to make sure I looked into this thoroughly because I couldn't see Kali doing no fuck shit like that. I hated being around snakes and liars, so I hope that my vibe wouldn't show, and she feel that shit.

"Latrell, what's on your mind son?" Granny mumbled not even taking her eyes off the TV. I knew that eventually she would pick up on my mood because I'd been stale as hell since I got back.

"Ain't nothing wrong with me, Gran Mae," I lied. She turned the volume down on the TV.

"Latrell, lie again. Boy, them voices over there in your head are so damn loud that I can't hear the TV!" she spat. I screwed my face up at her because she was talking crazy as hell.

"How can you hear me and I ain't said a word?" I retorted.

"That's the damn problem. You sitting there not saying a word. The silence is killing you boy. Now what's the problem?" she demanded rather than asked. I didn't want to give granny too many details because of course, she thought I was a damn truck driver, so I had to make sure I gave her just enough for some advice.

"Well, there's this girl that I was trying to get to know, and I call myself liking. I heard some bad things about her, and it's kind of bad. It makes a nigga not even want to continue pursuing her," I told Gran Mae.

"Son, we all know when you hear things sometimes it may not be any truth to it, right? So, before you just fly off the handle and stop something that just might be destined, you need to talk with that person and try to seek the truth, and then make your decision from there. What if you end things then you find out that what you heard ain't the truth? I trust you will make the right decision but why in the hell are you just now telling me about this?" she yelled, throwing a pillow at me. I busted out laughing.

"Man, granny, you know I was going to tell you eventually, but shit, now she may not even be worth me telling you about," I said, speaking the truth.

I cherished moments like this and it made a nigga's heart all mushy. The only lady that could make me soft was my granny. I don't know what I would do without her. We continued to watch TV and chill for the remainder of the night.

Kali

"Thank you for this, Kali. I just don't know who would do this to MJ," MJ's wife cried.

I had come over right after breakfast to drop her off some money so that she could take care of MJ's arrangements and to make sure their family was straight.

"I have my men on it, and soon as we find out something, I will let you now and whoever did this, I will make sure to it that they pay," I consoled her.

She was crying hysterically, and her nose was dripping onto my silk Versace shirt. I slid off the couch and planted a fake smile on my face, but bitch I was fuming on the inside. This was a two-thousand-dollar shirt, and now it was covered in salty tears and snot.

When I stepped outside the house, I headed straight to the trunk and popped it. Call me bougie or whatever you wanted to, but I kept an extra pair of everything in the trunk of my vehicles. I stood right there in broad daylight and removed the shirt I had on replacing it with another until I was able to head home and redo my outfit. My security surrounded me anyway, so it was no biggie. After changing, I headed to see my brother. Yeah, I was still pissed with him, but for him to not show his face with the shit that was going on wasn't right. That nigga would do anything to have first dibs on information if he knew he was about to be running something.

I pulled up at the house he shared with Myia and made my way to the entrance. I used the key that Myia had given me and let myself in. He didn't know I had a key. Walking in, I could hear his loud chuckle coming from the back where his office was at. I made my way down the long hallway and stood outside the door for a few to see if I could catch anything off from his conversation. Realizing nothing unusual was being said, I twisted the knob and made my way inside. He looked up and his smile faded.

"Let me call you back," he told the caller. I rolled my eyes and stood there.

"Wassup sis, I for sure thought you weren't talking to me for a while?" he laughed. I kept my poker face on because clearly, I didn't see shit funny.

"This ain't that type of visit brother. Have you heard about MJ?" I asked. Kalicio scratched his head and let out a sigh.

"I've been busy so nah wassup?" he said.

"You been so busy getting your shit off the ground that you just been moving foul all the way around, huh? Well, since you don't know MJ was found dead yesterday. He was stabbed to death, and then whoever did it place a counterfeit bill on him as if they were trying to send a message!" I spat. I moved around and finally took a seat in the chair.

I could tell that news hit my brother hard because MJ was OG, so he was like a father figure to my brother at times.

"Shit," he hissed and punched his fist.

"I've already been to his house and gave his family some money. The streets ain't talking yet, so it's hard to find anything out right now. This shit is just baffling because I'm not beefing with anyone, so I don't know who the hell is fucking with me," I rambled. I looked up at my brother and chewed on my bottom lip.

"You ain't been on no dumb shit, have you?" I flat out asked.

"Really KK, hell nah. I would never bring no heat your way. You straight though, you got everything covered?" he asked.

My phone started to ring, and I reached into my bag and removed it, looking at the screen. It was Synzari.

"I got to take this but yeah I'm always straight," I told my brother before walking out of his office. Answering the phone, I walked back through the house and to my car.

"Hello," I said quickly.

"So, you ready for our outing because a nigga got to take advantage of this downtime?" he asked. A smile graced my face.

"Sure, do I need to come to you or what?" I asked.

"Nah I want to cater to you, I can scoop you," he said.

I debated on whether or not I wanted to give him my address to my crib, but I looked down at my clothes and realized I needed to change so yeah, he was going to have to come to the house.

"Ok, I'll shoot you my address because I need to change. Don't try no slick shit because you won't make it out the gate," I told him. I could hear him smack his lips through the phone.

"Girl whatever, but aite I'll see you in about an hour. I know how females take all day getting ready," he said.

"Bye, nigga," I said, hanging up the phone.

I couldn't contain my excitement I was excited to see what Synzari's fine ass had to offer. I know I was hitting NASCAR speeds trying to get home.

KALICIO

The news that KK delivered was a low blow. This shit was already coming back on me because I knew MJ murder had something to do with Premium. This nigga was probably sending a message, and if he was doing that, it meant he was sending somebody for my ass and KK too. My intentions with Premium were to get put on, and that was it. The transaction was a one-time thing. Good thing no one knew where my traps or blocks were at. I knew Myia needed her space, but I also had to make sure she kept her mouth closed. A woman scorn is one that shouldn't be fucked with. I was going to make arrangements for dinner to be prepared and have a romantic night, something that we haven't done in a long time.

I continued to rub my temples to try to relieve some of the stress that burdened me. Opening the desk drawer, I removed the phone that I used for Premium. After checking the phone, it showed exactly what I knew would be on there— missed calls and messages from Premium and July. I removed the battery and smashed the phone on the desk before tossing it in the trash.

It was time to move around, but before I left, I called up the florist and order Myia some of her favorite flowers to have delivered to her today. Smiling at my gesture, I knew Myia ass was gone be hard to break. That was the one thing that drew me to her. She ain't take no shit.

Leaving the house, I checked my surroundings and made sure nothing looked out of the way. Once the coast was clear, I hopped in my truck. I kept throwaway phones in the glove box, so I reached in and grabbed one. Placing a call to my trap, I gave them directions to be discreet and send someone to link with me for an update. I wasn't going to go directly to the trap just in case somebody was watching me. I gave orders to meet me at China Village.

I made it to Ewing Lane in fifteen minutes tops. I walked in and placed me an order of beef & broccoli and a couple of egg rolls. While I waited on my food, I watched as my worker pulled up. He got out the car with a backpack and made his way into the restaurant as if he was ordering food. I took a seat at a nearby table, and once he placed his food order, he came over and took a seat.

"Shit, what's up mane, why you meeting me in a random ass place?" he asked.

"Does it matter?" was all I said. He placed the backpack on the floor and slid it over to me.

"Look, make sure you keep everything discreet on the block. An issue popped up, and I got to make sure we low key. You seen anything out of the ordinary around the way?" I asked.

"Nah, everything is straight," he replied.

I heard some Chinese from behind, and I turned around to my food being placed on the counter. I grabbed the backpack and headed to grab my food. My mind was on some much shit that I had to move around. I couldn't sit in one place for a long period of time. I needed to switch cars and park my truck because everyone knew my truck. I dapped my homie up and left out.

When I got in the truck, I had a missed call from KK. I wondered what she wanted. I had already crossed her, but I slick needed to get back in with her so that she wouldn't think nothing more about me being distant. If I knew my sister, I knew that she was already feeling a way about how I been acting lately. She knew something was up.

"Wassup, KK?" I answered.

"Umm, I have a date," was all she said.

My sister wasn't big on dating, and she pretty much was a hit and run type of female. I know that sound niggerish, but that's just how she was. The only things she ever cared about were her business and money, so for her to call and say she had a date, she wanted me to be big brother. That shit actually made a nigga feel bad because I had done some of the most fucked up shit.

"Aw hell, with who?"

"Synzari."

"So what you want me to do? You feeling this nigga?" I asked.

"I mean I think I might like him. It's time I started trying to settle down. What do you think, I know you been kicking it with Premium lately?" she said, making me tense up.

"Just do what you always do, sis. Don't put all your trust into these niggas so easily. Motherfuckers are grimy. He be around Premium, but Syn is one of them keep to himself types, so I don't really know too much about him," I honestly told her.

"Well aite thanks big guy," she said. I could hear the smile in her voice. Closing my eyes and shaking my head, she was laying it on thick.

"I love you, KK," I told her.

"I love you too even though you're a complete asshole sometimes. You and Myia coming over tomorrow?" she asked.

"Shit, if I can get her to hear a nigga out, we will be there,"

"Ok, fingers crossed. Bye, I have to get ready for my date." She laughed. Just like that, we ended our call. I haven't even heard from Myia yet, and I knew that she had received my delivery by now.

Myia

SITTING HERE on the bed that Kalicio and me shared, I had been here a short while since I received his flowers. I knew I could be stubborn as hell sometimes, but I was just hurt and not feeling a lot of shit that he was doing. I wanted to make things work with him because he was my heart, but I was unclear about that. The dinner that was being prepared downstairs smelled good. I knew his ass wasn't going to cook, so he did what he did best and spent money to have somebody do it. Looking at the clock, I figured Kalicio would be here soon, so I got up and started to freshen up and get dressed for dinner.

I pulled a nice fitted dress out the closet that I knew would hug my curves. After freshening up and combing my hair, I walked out of the bathroom to Kalicio standing there. Our eyes met, and we held each other's gaze.

"How long you been here?" he asked.

"Long enough, thank you for the flowers," I told him, showing my appreciation for them.

"It was nothing. I owe you more than an apology, and I couldn't believe I was tripping the way I was tripping. Myia, I really apologize for what I did, and I swear you ain't got to worry about July nor any other months well hoes ever again. I just wanted everything to be perfect and run smoothly. So, I was blinded by what was right and wrong," he said

I took in his facial expressions seeing if I could read him. His body language was normal and nothing out of the ordinary.

"I accept it for now, but I'm still watching you because I don't trust that hoe July!" I spat. I walked over and placed a kiss on Kalicio lips. We kissed for what felt like forever, and this kiss felt different. I don't know what it was, but it didn't feel like the many other kisses we shared.

KALI

It had taken me forever to find something to wear. I wanted everything to be perfect. There was no way I could have Syn picking me up, and I'm looking bummish. That wasn't my style. I stood in front of the floor length mirror as I pulled my shirt over my head. Fluffing my hair out of my shirt, I ran my hands through my curls. I turned around and looked at my ass in the mirror, which was sitting up pretty in the jeans I wore. There was a knock at my bedroom door.

"Kali, your guest has arrived," Marisol said.

"Ok, tell him I'll be down in a minute!" I yelled over my shoulder.

I heard Marisol walk away and I walked over to my closet and grabbed a pair of Jimmy Choo heels that I been dying to wear. I finished off with spraying a few pumps of Jimmy Choo perfume. Satisfied, I headed downstairs to meet Synzari.

Making my way down the steps, I could see Synzari sitting on the couch with a drink in his hand. When my heels hit the marble floor, he turned around. The way he licked his lips made me smile. Shit, I think I was blushing hard.

"Sorry to keep you waiting." I smiled, making my way to take a seat beside him on the couch.

"It's all good. It was worth it, even though your fine ass could've walked down here in sweatpants and a t-shirt, and I still would've taken you out." He laughed. The way his lips touched the glass when he took another sip of the liquor made me lick my own lips.

"Getting an early start on drinking?" I asked.

"Something to take the jitters off." He shrugged.

"Why are you nervous, I'm just like any other girl you take out?" I told him. He shook his head.

"Girl, you are nothing like any gal I done took out. You're on a level by yourself. You might want to eat somewhere bougie where a nigga got to make reservations and shit, then talk about me to your friends." He chuckled and took another sip. I reached and took the glass out of his hand.

"Look, yeah, I might be on another level, but I'm not too good for anything you have planned. You asked me out, so I'm down for whatever you have planned. My bag hasn't always been secured. I struggled coming up like others. I'm feeling you for some reason, and that's rare for me. So, if I tell anything to my friends it will be how I meet this great man who took his time with me and lead the way, and I followed for a change," I truthfully spoke.

This nigga had me speaking deep at this point. We could have gone to McDonald's and got something off the value menu.

"Damn that's how you feel?" he asked. I nodded my head reassuring him. I took his glass that was now half full and chugged the rest of the contents.

"You ready?" I asked. He stood up and held his hand out for me to grab. Grabbing his hand, I stood to my feet.

"Yep," I said, looking in his eyes.

"Do you trust me?" he blurted out. I lifted my brow because I didn't know if I did and why was he asking me this.

"Why?" I curiously asked.

"Do you have to have your entire security team with you? If it's one thing I know is that I can protect you from anything so they won't be needed," he replied.

Lord, I didn't know how I felt about that one. I didn't go anywhere without my men. They weren't the type to overcrowd. You didn't even know they were there, especially if I'm out in a public setting.

"Synzari it's not that I don't trust you, but you have to understand this is our first date on top of that we done had some issues in my camp with a member of my team being murdered. We don't know who the hell did this, so I can't call my security off tonight. They won't be close. They always be discreet in public," I told him.

"That's fucked up. I've never known for you to be beefing with anybody. Is everything good?" he asked. I bit my bottom lip thinking if I should tell him anything. I found myself pillow talking and hell we weren't even in the damn bed yet.

"One thing about me is I'm not no drama type of chick. I have rules set in my organization so that shit like this doesn't happen. I really think MJ death was personal and someone is trying to send me a message because he was stabbed, and a hundred-dollar bill was pinned to his chest with the knife. So, this shit got me baffled and trying to find out what the hell is going on has slick stressed me out," I told him. He nodded his head.

"Well let me try to take your mind off all that by making you have a good time tonight," Syn said.

"Let's go!" I cheered excitedly.

Synzari

EVEN THOUGH I was here to take Kali out, the other half of me was still on a mission. I hated this shit because I really was feeling her ass. When she walked down the steps and took a seat beside me, her perfume was playing with a nigga's nose. One thing that stood out to me was how she answered regarding calling off her security off. When she said one of her crew members was killed, I knew it had Premium's name all on it. More than anything I didn't want to raise her suspicions by keep asking questions but how she seemed clueless as to why this was happening made my radar go off. She wasn't a sloppy person and ran her company with rules. Those rules were set so that nobody she did business with would be crossed. That alone made me think that Kali didn't have anything to do with this. I still had to look further because she could be just a good liar and telling me anything.

After we left Kali's house, I took her to Dave & Buster's. I wanted to see if she meant what she said. I wanted her to let loose and have fun, and that's exactly what we were going to do. We walked into Dave & Buster's hand in hand.

"You bowl?" I asked the look on her face was priceless. She pointed to the heels she had on.

"That ain't nothing. We can buy socks from here," I told her.

"Well, I'm down. You have to teach me how to though," she shyly said.

"I got you." I laughed.

I headed over to the counter, and she followed where I paid for our game and got our shoes. We walked over to our booth, and we sat down I reached down and grabbed Kali's feet, placing them in my lap.

"What are you doing?" she gasped.

"Relax, I'm putting your shoes on," I whispered.

I could feel how tense she was when I grabbed her foot. She relaxed, and I undid the straps on her shoes. I slowly removed each shoe and rubbed her soft feet. She got points for them bitches being pretty and polished. I slid her socks on. A nigga really hated to put these busted up ass bowling shoes on her feet, but we had to. I placed her shoes on and tied them both up.

"That was sweet of you," she whispered as if she was in a dream.

"Hello, I will be your server can I get you guys something to drink?" the guy asked. He couldn't keep his eyes off Kali, and I didn't like that shit.

"You talking to her or both of us?" I asked.

"I'm sorry I was talking to the both of you," he quickly replied.

"Check this out. You look at me, and I'll ask her what she wants and tell you. You standing up there eye fucking my date, and I don't take kindly to disrespect!" I spat.

I turned to Kali who I thought would be upset, but she had a smirk on her face as if she was enjoying every bit of it.

"Rémy and Sprite," she said. I turned back to him.

"Rémy and Sprite for her, and I want a Hennessey straight on the rocks. Keep them coming and throw in some wings and fries," I told him.

"I want some Nachos also," Kali blurted out.

"You heard the lady," I said, shooing him away. He walked off, and I turned to Kali.

"Sorry about that," I apologized.

"There was no need. You felt disrespected, so you spoke up. Don't think you have to change who you are around me. Now come on so that I can whoop your ass." She stood up.

"I thought you said I had to teach you?" I asked.

"I was just playing. I can bowl. You want to make a wager?" she asked.

"Oh, you that good, now you want to bet and shit? Man, I don't know that depends what you are betting,"

"You scared, it's ok. How about we bowl one game then you can decide if you want to bet or not?"

"Aite cool."

I didn't know what she wanted to bet, but I bet one thing I was going to break her down by the end of the night.

PREMIUM

I had Syn on Kali and Kalicio, but I had my young niggas from the streets handling members from their team. It was nothing to catch them coming from work and snatch them up. I had put out another hit for another member of her crew to be handled. I could care less if she had two people standing bout time I got done with them. I sat there in my office just staring into space and replaying the conversations that Kalicio and I had in my head repeatedly. I bet this nigga had taken the lead in all of this, but the fact that Kali allowed him to do it and her name was used made her just as guilty as he was.

I was just waiting on the call and a picture of the dirty work. That nigga Kalicio had got ghost. The number I had for him was disconnected. He wasn't even seen out in public. He was just laying low, but I knew he was making money. He wasn't gone interfere with his profit. That's why I'm glad I had Synzari because he getting close to Kali would get him close to Kalicio and his whereabouts. This nigga didn't even know his enemy was closer than he imagined.

My phone buzzed, and I quickly grabbed it. It was picture mail, and I click on it fast as hell. The sight of yet another one of Kali's crew members dead was making my dick hard. It was done just right, and the bill was placed in the exact same spot as that nigga MJ. An evil smile spread across my face, and I placed the phone down. Letting out an evil laugh, I was satisfied.

Kali

WE SAT in the driveway of my house listening to music and having conversation. I was enjoying myself so much that I didn't even want to go in yet. We had been sitting out here for I know about an hour. I had whooped his ass in three games of bowling and we had drunk so much liquor that I'm glad that we even made it home safely. This date wasn't about how much money he had spent, but the fact that he was able to get all the way out my comfort zone and have the best time I had had in a long time was everything.

"So, it's just you and your brother?" he asked. My head was leaned back against the seat because that bitch was spinning. I had way too much Rémy.

"Yeah, but lately he been moving a little off for me. I feel us slipping further apart. He has a hard time working under me. I think he has this complex about a woman being able to run something so big, so he feels as if I be dogging him because he's a worker. He's trying to venture off and do his own shit that I don't want no parts of. He's just been secretive as hell. At the end of the day, that's still my brother. I raised him," I said.

"That's what family is for. Do you think he would ever do anything to hurt you and your business?" Syn asked which made me look at him like he was crazy.

"I don't know. When we fuss, we be saying some hurtful shit to each other, but we always make back up. I don't think he would do nothing crazy," I whispered. Even though I answered, I was really asking myself that in my head because would Kalicio ever cross me.

"I want you," I heard Syn whisper. He leaned over the seat and placed his hand in my hair. I knew he was a bit tipsy because hell I

KYEATE

was, but my hormones were raging, and I wanted him to in the worse way.

"We're grown. I want you too," I let it escape my lips. I leaned closer to his face and placed my lips against his. The kiss got so hot that I didn't know if he had turned the heat on in here or not. I placed my hand on his chest pushing him away.

"My bad," he said.

"Come in," I told him, reaching for the door handle.

I skipped up the steps like a happy kid unlocking the door. I watched as Syn made his way in the house and I locked the door behind him. We both laughed and headed upstairs to my bedroom.

"This motherfucker is big," he said, looking around my room.

I slowly undid my shirt pulling it over my head. I was standing there in my bra and jeans. When Syn turned back around, he licked his lips and signaled for me to come towards him. Slowly walking towards him, I felt my heartbeat increase. Syn sat down on the bench that I had in front of my bed. He placed his hands on my waist and looked me in my eyes.

"Take these jeans off, but leave them heels on," he demanded.

I undid my jeans and slowly pulled them down. Turning my back to him, I used his body as leverage as I bent over and pulled the jeans over my heels. I slanged the jeans across the room, and I stood before him in only in my underwear and a pair of Jimmy Choos. Walking over to him, I lifted his arms and pulled his shirt over his head. His tatted chest turned me on even more. Straddling him, my lips met his once again to ignite the fire that we made in the car. The way his hands roamed all over my body, I was ready to fuck him in the worse way. Hell, I wanted my dick sucked and didn't even have one.

He grabbed me and lifted me as he carried me to the bed. Laying me down, he had a hungry glare in his eyes. He stuck his fingers inside the lace of my panties and inserted them inside of me. I let out a small moan. The way he was working my insides made me want more. I started grinding into his fingers, and he pulled them out. After he snatched my panties off, he dove headfirst into the ocean that awaited him. The way his tongue felt on my flesh, I had a grip on the sheets.

Syn knew what he was doing. When he lifted his head and locked eyes with me, I could see my juices glistening on his beard. He removed his boxers and placed himself between my legs. Planting his lips on mine, he slowly inserted himself inside of me. Now I could tell that Syn didn't have the biggest dick, but he was working me. His strokes started gently, and he was touching me the right way because my eyes started rolling back into my head. My mind was blown I wanted to get on top, so I patted his chest signaling for him to get up. He laid down, and I climbed on top taking in his size. As I said I knew it wasn't huge, but it was perfect, and the girth was on point. I slowly eased down on top and enjoyed the ride of a lifetime. I was very flexible and could get in all kinds of positions while riding, which made me realize that Syn couldn't hold his composure for long. He quickly lifted me up, put me on all fours, and slid back in me from behind where we finished off with a blast.

We laid there in the ambiance trying to catch our breath. I didn't know what was going through his head, but I was scared at what was going through mine. I was liking everything about him, and him being able to satisfy me sexually was the icing on the cake.

"If you run off on me, I will have to have you killed," I joked as I ran my hands across his chest.

"Never that, so you basically feeling the kid, huh?" he asked.

"I must say that I am and that's rare for me. I'm scared I have never been in a real relationship since I got my business off the ground. I'm used to satisfying my needs and sending niggas on their way. I don't want to run you off," I admitted.

"We just have to do things together, day by day. This shit is new to me too," he said.

The feeling of being in his arms made me feel complete. He kissed the top of my head, and I closed my eyes. I let sleep take over me while I was safe in his arms.

KALICIO

Last night with Myia was great, and we had put a lot of things on the table regarding our relationship. Dinner was great, and hell dessert was even better if you know what I'm saying up until I received a phone call that another one of KK's members had been found dead after work. This shit was coming back so fast on a nigga that I didn't have time to process shit. We tried calling KK's ass, but she wasn't answering no damn phone calls. Myia sat in the passenger side with tears running down her face. I hated to see her cry and to know that this shit was all my fault was fucked up. Myia was close to all the workers. They worked together every day, so she was taking this hard.

I pulled up to my sister's house and noticed that nigga Syn's car was still outside. This why her ass couldn't answer because she was probably laid up with this nigga. Myia and I hopped out the car, and soon as I made it to the porch, Marisol opened the door.

"Good morning y'all. Kali hasn't come down yet," she said.

"That's all good. This is an emergency," I said, skipping up the steps.

"She has male company!" Marisol shouted. I shrugged my shoulders because I didn't give a fuck.

I turned the knob on the door, and it was unlocked. Walking into the room with Myia on my tail KK was laid all in this nigga's arm dead at the world. I walked over to the edge of the bed and tapped KK on the foot.

"KK!" I shouted. As soon as the last K left my mouth, this nigga Syn had a gun pointed at me.

"What the fuck, nigga!" I yelled. KK stirred and opened her eyes. Her eyes landed on me then to Syn who was still aiming the gun.

"What the hell is going on? Why you in my bedroom, and why do you have a gun pointed at my brother?" she asked in confusion. Syn lowered the gun.

"My bad, all I heard was somebody shouting your name. I'm always TTG." He shrugged placing the gun back on the bedside table.

"We've been fucking blowing your phone up all night and you up here laid up when shit done got real again!" I spat. KK grabbed her phone.

"It was off but don't come in here talking that shit, you know how to fucking get in touch with me if you can't reach my cell. Kalicio, stop acting brand new. Now what the fuck is the problem?" she yelled back.

This exactly the shit I be talking about she doesn't know how to talk to a man. She speaks to a nigga like I'm her child.

"Another body was found, the same exact way." I sighed. Myia started crying again.

"The fuck, who the fuck keeps doing this shit and why!" she yelled throwing the covers back and getting out the bed. KK was ass naked, and she didn't give a shit who saw her. She walked to the bathroom and slammed the door.

"We'll be downstairs!" I yelled at her and left the room with Myia. I took a seat on the couch, and a nigga was antsy. My nerves were getting the best of me. I needed to check on my spots.

Kali entered the living room with her housecoat on, and she started to pace the floor.

"Who was it?" she asked with concern all over her face. I honestly didn't want to tell her because I knew she would be hurt by this one.

"Lil Chris," I sighed. She closed her eyes shut and tapped her head with hand balled up.

"I'm trying my hardest to figure out what the hell is going on and why somebody is coming for my team. Did they leave the money also like on MJ?" she asked. I nodded my head yes.

"It's some shit going on inside of my organization. It's a snake somewhere in this bitch. Call an emergency meeting in an hour. Myia write a check for Chris' family also let them know I will continue his mother's treatments. You can drop it to his family after the meeting," KK ordered. She stormed out of the room. She was pissed.

Synzari

I had the perfect shot for that nigga, but I couldn't act that fast. I can tell this shit was bothering Kali, which did nothing but prove to me she ain't know her own brother was a snake and Premium was knocking her people off left and right and he wasn't going to stop either. Kali came marching back in the room, plopped down on the bed, and she placed her head in her hands.

Everything good?" I asked. I wanted to tell her so bad, but I couldn't.

"It's a snake on my team, and I'm going to find out who is bringing this heat to me. I don't step on nobody's toes, and now somebody wants to step all on mine. I'm even good to all my employees, so the fact that somebody done did some foul shit makes me not trust anyone," she said. I rubbed her back.

"Everything that's done in the dark always comes to light," was all the advice I could offer.

"Thanks for a good time yesterday. I'm not putting you out, but I have a meeting, and I need to get this shit handled," she told me.

"Oh, you stuck with me now. Anyway, I got shit to handle too but we most definitely linking later. If you need me, just hit me up,"

Kali leaned in and kissed me, her minty lips locking with mine I didn't want to leave.

"I like the sound of that," she whispered.

As soon as I left Kali's house, I headed straight to see Premium. The thing about Premium he wasn't going to back out of this shit. He had already crossed the line. I just hope that I don't have to take this nigga out myself. I parked and reached in my glove box for my other gun. I wasn't stepping foot in here not strapped. Hopefully, things don't even get that heated. Premium knew how I rocked. Opening the door, I eased out of the car and made my way inside. I gave everyone a head nod that was sitting out front and made my way on to the back. I knocked on the door. I could hear Premium on the phone.

"Come in!" he yelled.

Walking in, I took a seat in the chair and allowed him to finish his phone call. He held his hand up letting me know that he would be a minute.

"Yeah, same exact thing in twenty-four hours. I don't care you will do it until I say stop!" he spat and slammed the phone down on the desk.

"Sorry bout that, what's up, Syn?" he greeted me.

"Why are you trying to get a war going by dropping all these people from Kali's team?" I just flat out asked. Premium leaned up in his chair and laughed.

"How I handle the rest of my business isn't your concern. I'm paying you to handle what I want you to handle, speaking of which, what's the latest?"

"I know Kali ain't your girl. Kalicio name is all on this. I haven't figured out just yet why he would throw his sister under the bus, but she is clueless as hell as to what's going on. She's got a meeting in a minute because she said that it's a snake in her camp and this is why all this shit is happening," I told Premium. He sat there for a minute.

"I can't see Kalicio doing his sister like that. This nigga came to me saying Kali wanted this shit and was going to let him run it. Now the money I got was fake as hell, and she runs that shit, so she's guilty by association," he shrugged.

"What association? Premium, now you know I done got in close with her, so she's been open about some things. This she has nothing to do with it. I will take Kalicio out once I get factual proof that Kali is innocent," I told him.

"Oh, so that's why you here, you done got some pussy now want to save your hoe. Listen here, if you don't kill Kali when you kill Kalicio I'll just have somebody else do it." He shrugged. I stood up and looked at him like he was crazy.

"Watch what I tell you, she innocent!" I spat before walking out.

I needed a way to get close to Kalicio and try to get in his head about what was going on. This shit was getting messier and messier.

KALI

It was early as hell, and I sat here sipping on Henn overlooking the floor as everyone made their way into the warehouse.

"Snake ass motherfuckers," I hissed.

Taking another sip from the glass, I held the liquid in my mouth and let it burn the inside of my cheeks before swallowing it. I looked at my watch, and it was almost meeting time. Walking away from the window, I made my way out of my office and slowly walked down the hall. I felt the presence of my two heavy hitters walking behind me. I wanted them here in case I ordered for somebody to be handled. Normally I loved to hear my heels walking down this hall, but today, I was rocking tennis shoes, which was rare for me. I had my hair pulled back in a ponytail. I basically didn't give a shit because if I had to get down and dirty, I would. One of my guys opened the door, and I walked into a rowdy room. Everyone was carrying on conversations. I stood in front of the table and slammed the glass so hard that it broke. Liquor splashed everywhere, but I didn't care.

Looking around the table, I looked at everybody like a snake, even my own brother. I started to speak.

"As you guys know we have had a couple of losses over the past few days. If I'm right, those will not be the last. So, that brings us here. Somebody in this room or one of them motherfuckers that is dead, God rest their soul, has crossed this organization bringing heat to my front door. I'm not going to ask what the rules are because you motherfuckers know. I used to think I could trust everyone here, but I don't know who to trust. Somebody wants to bring everything that I worked for down, but why. I wish I knew the answer. I pay all you guys more than enough. I respect you all, and this is the thanks I get. Yeah, the street code is no snitching, but if you cared anything about Chris and MJ, somebody had better start singing. I want to know whatever. If anything fishy has been going on around here that I don't know about, speak now, or taste the steel of this piece," I said, placing my gun on the table. Still looking around the room, everyone was looking at each other. Kalicio sat on his phone.

"Ms. Kali, I can only speak for myself, and I have my daughters to raise. I can't afford to be looking over my back or scared to leave work thinking someone may do me like they did Chris and MJ. The only thing that came through here that wasn't legit was the order that Kalicio requested. He put a rush on it, so it was practically a bad batch," Griselda whispered.

My neck damn near snapped looking at Kalicio. Now he looked up from his phone with his mouth wide opened.

"What the fuck is she talking about?" I spat.

"She tripping, I had them do an order, but it wasn't used for nothing but strip club shit. I needed it because I hadn't got my shit off yet. I had used the majority of my money to get plugged in," he told me.

I kept my eyes on my brother. He had a hellafied poker face, but I felt he was lying because this nigga wasn't broke. He ate like I ate, and I ain't in the streets like that, but a nigga like Kalicio Kusain wouldn't go broke buying drugs. I looked over at Myia.

"You knew about this?" I asked.

"Yeah, I wasn't going to do it, but he came in here demanding shit. I didn't know what it was for," she said while she gave Kalicio an evil look. I thought back to that day that I found that balled up sheet on the floor.

"You ain't exchange that money with nobody, right Kalicio?" I asked.

"No, I didn't. Why in the hell would I do some shit like that KK? Hell, that's like signing my own death certificate. I ain't no snake!" he shouted.

"Who the fuck you yelling you at?" I said, walking over to him.

"Man go head on, KK. You sit up in here and talk to a motherfucker any kind of way then get butthurt when somebody yells at you. I will forget you my sister and treat you like one of these bitches on the street." The venom in his voice was evident. I started laughing.

"A hit dog will holler, huh? Why the fuck you always bitching about how you getting talked to. Is that why you wanted to get your own shit started because you can't handle orders from a bitch? Nigga, I raised your big ass. I changed your diapers and had your back. If you wanted to be king of anything, you wouldn't have been begging for me to put you on. *Let me work under you, Kali. I'll make sure nothing ever happens to you, Kali,*" I said, mocking his voice. He stood up facing me, and my two heavy hitters were right by my side.

"Ok, chill out y'all. This has gone too far— y'all sitting here beating up on each other when y'all need to come together and figure out who is behind this. We can't stop detail because of this. This has put us behind a day on orders," Myia spoke up sounding like the voice of reasoning.

She was right my own brother had gotten reckless with me, and that shit burned like hell. I turned to everyone else.

"Nobody is to leave this warehouse alone. You will be escorted home or wherever until I find out what's going on. You are being watched so don't try no fuck shit," I demanded.

As everyone got up to leave, I looked at my brother again shaking my head. I couldn't believe we had come to this point.

KALICIO

KK had her motherfucking nerve questioning me in front of everybody and Griselda with her old dry snitching ass. I didn't have a choice but to flip out on KK so that I could make her think I was innocent. I was wrong for saying some of the shit that I said to her though. Shaking my head at my thoughts, I was making this shit bigger and digging a deeper hole for myself. I would never come back from this, and I know once KK finds out that I really was behind this, she would wipe her hands of me.

Pulling up in my driveway, I turned the car off and sat there for a minute. I could feel Myia's eyes on me. I heard her open the door.

"I'm going to go warm you up something to eat," she said and climbed out of the truck.

As soon as she got out, I reached into the ashtray and lit the blunt that I had there. I took that shit to the head. It wasn't a high that could soothe me right now. I tossed the blunt out the window and made my way in the house. Headed straight to my office, I walked in and closed the door calling my right hand to check on the traps. He picked up on the first ring.

"Wassup, nigga?" he said.

"Listen it's a lot of shit going down, and I need you to keep your ears to the street and watch out for that nigga Premium. He's got it out for me right now because of that fake batch to get that work, and he not going to stop until he finds me. I'm going to be laying low for a while, I got a few loose ends to tie up then I'm going to head out of town," I rambled off. I turned around in my chair and looked out the window into the backyard.

"He's been snooping around. I don't know if word done got out that you serving over this way, but it's been some crackhead asking about you,"

"Man aite, just remember what I said. Also, if anybody come around asking about my sister, you don't know nothing!" I spat.

When I turned back around in my chair, Myia was standing there with tears running down her face. I quickly hung up the phone. She slammed the plate she was holding on my desk.

"Please tell me you didn't lie to me and that you didn't do your own blood like that?" she yelled. I wasn't sure how much she had heard.

"Baby, what you talking bout?" I stuttered.

"Stop fucking lying and acting like you don't know shit. You had me make that bad batch, and you gave that shit to Premium. You told him Kali wanted in, so that's why she's taking heat because he thinks this shit is on her when really it was your dumb ass. Something is truly wrong with you. It's like I don't even know who you are anymore. What did Kali ever do to you?" she cried. It was no point in lying anymore because she had heard everything.

"Myia, you would never understand being in somebody shadow. I used Kali name because her name holds weight," I admitted.

"So, you wanted to venture out on your own but couldn't be man enough to do it on your own. You make like you so tired of being in KK's shadow, but yet you use her name to help you get on. That's some weak ass shit Kalicio, and you know it!" she spat.

"Go head on Myia, kissing and running behind KK ass!" I yelled. She stood there and shook her head at me. She stepped forward, and I leaned back in the chair because she was liable to tag a nigga with her crazy ass.

"When I leave out this house Kalicio, I will not return. This, what we had is done, but I'm going to leave you being honest with your sister all on you. I know you will never be man enough to tell her what it is that you done. You just better hope your karma don't come before you get to tell her," she said with so much pain in her voice.

I didn't have anything to say. Myia walked out of my office and my life.

Myia

Today had been the longest day of my life. I hated to get in between a family squabble, but if I didn't jump in when I did KK and Kali would've come to blows up in there. I thought I was going to come home, feed my man, and then get my back blown out, but what I walked in on changed that. I couldn't believe what I had heard. I would have never thought Kalicio would cross his own sister like that. That man had a special kind of hate in his heart for Kali, and she never knew. Walking out on him was the best decision that I could make, but there was no way that I could face Kali knowing what I knew. I felt obligated to tell her, but I felt that type of betrayal she needed to hear from the source.

Walking into our bedroom, I grabbed me some clothes and threw them in a suitcase. It was nothing to get more things, but I would come back later. After grabbing my personal toiletries, I threw them in the bag and headed back downstairs. Kalicio was standing at the bar fixing him a drink. He probably was about to drink himself to death.

"I'm gone, I'll be back to get the rest of my things sometime later," I told him. His stare was blank and didn't hold any emotion.

"Whatever Myia, just get out. You wanted to leave then you do that but you ain't coming back up in here. I don't care what you left behind," he seethed.

"That's where you wrong because I will be back. Did you forget this house is just as much as mine as it is yours? I just don't want to stay here with your lying disloyal ass. You talking to me like I'm crazy, but clearly you forgot who the fuck I was!" I yelled.

Kalicio sucked his teeth and shooed me away. I was not about to fight him again today. I was tired. Turning on my heels, I continued out before it came to just that.

SYNZARI

Kali was on her way over to my crib. It was out of the norm to let a female know where I laid my head, that's how I knew I was feeling her on another level. I had picked up us something to eat from Prince's Chicken. A nigga had been wanting hot chicken all day. Looking at my watch, I decided to sit down and catch a little bit of the game that was on. Turning on the TV, I tuned into the game. The ringing of my phone broke my attention. It was Premium calling.

"What?" I answered.

"I got a location on that nigga Kalicio, I'm going to shoot you a text, and you need to handle that asap," he ordered.

"Yeah whatever," I said, and hung up the phone.

My doorbell started to ring, so I clicked on my cameras and saw that it was Kali. I walked over to the door and answered it. She stood there dressed all the way down and looking as if she was stressed out. I didn't like that at all.

"Sup bae," I greeted her and moved over to let her inside. She walked in, and I closed the door. She stood there, and she just fell in my arms.

"What's wrong?" I asked as she just held on to me for dear life.

KALI KUSAIN

"It's just been one of them days," she whispered. I kissed the top of her head and pulled her over to the couch.

"Have you eaten? I got some Prince's in there," I asked.

"Nah, I'll eat later. I really don't have much of an appetite," she responded. I wanted to know just what was bothering her.

"How did the meeting go?" I threw out there. She let out a huge sigh and rolled her eyes.

"Basically, a bunch of nothing. Nobody knew shit about what was going on. Then one of my workers mentioned Kalicio ordering them to do a bad batch. So, I asked him about, and he says he used it for strip club purposes. That shit didn't even sound right to me. So shit, I spoke my peace on it, and this nigga went apeshit. Some words were said, and if Myia hadn't interfered, we probably would've come to blows in there. He just said a lot of shit that I didn't know about. This whole time I thought I was helping him by putting him on, but he slick resents me for that. I had to remind him that I was the one that raised him. He was too disrespectful," she confided in me.

As I listened to the things that she was saying, I thought if only she knew why her brother was all defensive, and it was simply because his ass almost got busted. That's aite. I was going to get the truth out of him before I killed his ass.

"That's fucked up that all of this is pulling y'all both apart when y'all need to be coming together. Real shit though, how do you think you would feel if it came back that your brother was behind all this? Would you want him dead for crossing you and putting your life in danger? It's a lot that comes with that just keep doing what you doing and get them squares out ya circle. You don't want that type of company around you, blood or not," I said.

"I don't even know how I would process that honestly, but you're right. I guess I have to get down and dirty to weed out the bad guy, but I don't want to put a damper on our night either sitting here talking about it," she laughed.

"I have to leave out in the morning on business for about two days. It's some last-minute shit I got to handle. So, I'm about to warm up my chicken, you gone eat or not?" I joked standing up from the couch.

"I'll eat, baby. Then I want some dessert," she said sexily. I adjusted my dick in my pants because I knew what she was referring to and I didn't mind giving it to her.

I went into the kitchen and warmed up the food bringing it back to the living room. She had removed her shoes and was sitting comfortably on the floor in front of the table. She looked so innocent with her hair in a ponytail on top of her head. I sat her food down in front of her and placed mine beside hers. A nigga grabbed a piece of skin from the chicken and popped it in my mouth, and when I looked over at her, she had her head bowed and was praying. I felt niggerish as hell for that. Once she finished, we both dug in together demolishing our chicken. The rest of the night we laid up and watched TV, well mostly the TV watched us because we had got wrapped up in conversation getting to know each other a little more. We were able to get bout a good hour in until Kali hopped on top of a nigga and took my dick.

* * *

SLOWLY OPENING MY EYES, I looked around and realized I was in bed. Looking to my side, I was in bed alone. I felt around underneath the covers looking for my boxers since I didn't have them on. I spotted them on the floor beside the bed, and I got up and grabbed them. When I went to grab my phone, I spotted a folded sheet of paper with my name on it. I instantly grabbed it because I knew Kali had left it by the girly writing.

Syn,

Thank you for taking my mind off the things of yesterday. I love that I can talk to you about anything. I didn't want to wake you because you looked so peaceful. Whenever you get back in town, I'll be waiting on you.

~Kali

THIS GIRL WAS ABOUT to become wifey if she kept on. Things were all good now, but when she gets wind of her brother being dead, I don't know how long I can keep that secret from her. Putting the letter in my drawer, I got up and headed to shower. I always had to go to work with a clear head. I needed nothing on my mind right now, not even Kali. Once I zoned out, it was no coming back until my mission was complete. While in the shower, I went over in my head what I wanted to do with Kalicio. He was going to be an easy mark, and I was doing shit my way not trying to leave no message for Kali and her crew like Premium had been doing. He wanted to do all this mystery murder shit, but that shit was for the birds.

After my shower, I headed to my closet and grabbed a pair of black jeans and a black t-shirt, making sure to top it off with a black hoodie and black Nikes. I hit the latch on my secret spot I had hidden in the closet and pressed the code to my safe. When I opened the safe, I grabbed my gun I used and placed it in the duffle bag. Before I left the house, I pulled the address up that Premium sent me. This must had been where he stayed at because it was a residential area. I knew I was going to have to watch the traffic of the place because I didn't need any more casualties. Making sure that I had everything, it was time to ride out. This nigga Kalicio was about to be done.

MYIA

Here I was sitting in a hotel that I came to last night. I was trying my best to stay low until I figured out what I wanted to do. I was running the warehouse from the cameras on my phone because I didn't want to run into Kali because then I would have to tell her the truth, and I wanted to give Kalicio time to do that. I laid back on the bed and just stared at the ceiling. Times like this I wish I had family to lean on or go to. I wasn't hurting for any cash, but for right now, I didn't want to splurge until I knew what I was going to do.

You ever been so deeply involved with someone that you never envision the turmoil that might come because you're just riding on a blissful wave? The least I ever expected from Kalicio was cheating, and even then, that wasn't until now. He made me feel whole, loved and all the things that a lost girl wanted to feel, then one bad turn just changed all that in the blink of an eye.

Kali wasn't going to take this well at all, and she was so close to the truth, closer than she thought. I just hope that she will understand why I didn't tell her right away. I did the right thing by leaving now. If I had of stayed with Kalicio, then I could understand if she felt I betrayed her.

Kali

When I left Synzari's house this morning, I didn't want to leave him at all. I felt so safe and comfortable being around him. I didn't want to come in and start getting clingy. The one thing I didn't question him about was his line of work. I knew it was street related, and the less you knew was how we operated in the streets. At least we made it through the night without losing another team member.

I had made it back home, and after showering, I was sitting comfortably in the middle of my bed just finishing a FaceTime call with my cousin in Peru. I was planning a trip out there because it was time for my yearly meeting that I would attend because, in this business, we had to stay on top of any changes and important news and devices so that I could bring that shit back to the states. I had to let my connect know that we had run into some beef that I was trying to handle. I wasn't about to let my organization crumble because somebody wanted to be a damn snake. I had my guys on this shit so hard that I was bound to come up with a name. Whoever was playing with me was going to pay dearly and wish that they had of researched me thoroughly.

The intercom came on interrupting me from my thoughts.

"Ms. Kali, Canton is here to see you?" Marisol's said.

"You can send him up." I sighed. I haven't really talked to Canton lately. He had been out of town for a little bit. There was a slight knock at the door, and looking over there, I saw him peek his head in.

"What are you peeking your head in for?" I asked him. He had the biggest smile on his face.

"I didn't know if you were decent or not. You don't usually just hang in bed like that," he said as he walked over and removed his shoes taking a seat on the bed beside me.

For some reason, I thought about Syn and how this wasn't cool. I knew Canton didn't know about him, so hopefully, he wouldn't try anything.

"It's just been a lot going on lately, and I haven't really had any rest, so I'm enjoying the bed."

"I heard about all that shit that went down. That's real fucked up about Chris. I know his mama ain't taking that well," Canton reminded me. I shook my head because every time I thought of Chris, that shit hurt me. He was young and trying to take care of his family.

"You know I'm still trying to wrap my head around all of this. Canton you know everybody eats and ain't no ill will in my company, so I just don't know who snaking me," I admitted.

"What Kalicio got to say about all this?" he asked. I rolled my eyes at hearing his name.

"Fuck him. He's on some other shit. Shit got so bad with us that Myia had to get in between us," I told Canton.

"KK now you know I ain't the one to get into family matters, but that shit was bound to happen. Kalicio issues with you are something that he can only work out. I don't never have too much to say to him since he had an issue with the position you gave me." Canton shrugged.

I got silent and stared at the TV that was playing but was muted because I wasn't really watching it.

"I like somebody," I blurted out. Telling him about Syn was sitting on my mind. It was only right because the things that we were doing would no longer happen. Canton scratched his head.

"That was random. You think it will get serious KK because you don't get serious with nobody? Look how long we've been fucking around?" He laughed.

"It has a possibility of being serious. I really like him. He likes me also," I mumbled.

For some reason, I felt bad because Canton was right. We been fucking around for so long that he should've been the one I had given a chance with this relationship thing,

"Shit, I can't do nothing but respect that. It's a huge step for you, so

I wish you nothing but the best. Now who is it?" he asked, lifting his brow. I looked down at my phone and ignored his question.

"Kali, don't start. How you gone bring up the shit and then when I ask who it is get quiet? It must be some bum ass nigga." He laughed. I felt insulted.

"Nigga, do I look like the type of bitch that would date a bum ass nigga? For your information, it's this guy name Syn!" I spat. I could tell he was over there trying to place the name.

"Syn, Syn," he whispered. His eyes got big.

"Synzari?" he asked. I kept a straight face not wanting to get excited.

"You know him?" I asked.

"I don't know him personally, but I done seen him around," Canton said. There was an awkward silence.

"Let me eat you out one last time?" he quickly blurted out. This nigga here.

"Canton, now I wasn't going to ask you leave, but if you can't control yourself, then you got to go. This box is off limits." I laughed.

"I mean damn you ain't even official yet and already being faithful. He ain't got to know," Canton whispered as he leaned closer to me.

Now one thing about Canton he was a beast in the bedroom so me trying to fight him off right now was like trying to walk through a damn tornado.

"Canton, please stop," I whispered as he placed his lips on my neck. The motherfucker knew that was my damn spot. I started shaking my head because I wasn't a weak bitch and I wasn't about to go there with him.

"Canton, get out!" I yelled, moving my neck from him. He pulled away looking shocked, and I shrugged my shoulders. He had ten seconds to get the hell out of here, or he would be tossed out.

"Damn, you serious? You got me all hard and shit," he moaned.

"As a fucking heart attack and you got your own self all hard because I told your ass to stop. Please don't make this situation we had a hard one. I value your friendship and work relationship, but if you can't control your urges, then we going to have a problem," I told him.

Canton nodded his head and slid out of my bed. I watched as he put his shoes back on and then he stood to look at me.

"Sorry for all that, I'm going to head to the warehouse anyway and do night shift because can't nobody get in touch with Myia," he told me, raising a red flag. Where the hell was Myia ass?

"Aite, I'll try to give her a call," I told him.

Canton left, and I tried calling Myia from my cell. There was no answer. I didn't want to call Kalicio, but this was business.

SYNZARI

I had been sitting outside of Kalicio crib for a hot lil minute. The car that I knew Myia drove wasn't here. There wasn't no traffic at all, so it would be easy for me to get inside. I wasn't going to knock on the door because I wanted to talk to him before I killed him, and I couldn't risk being on camera. First thing I was going to do was sweep the grounds and check outside for any cameras. I pulled the hoodie over my head and grabbed my gun. The street was quiet, but I still made sure to watch my back. I got out the car and ran across the street.

A huge bush covered his mailbox, so I dipped behind it. When I looked at his yard, this shit was wide open, and the best thing that I could do was walk up the driveway slowly because it was darker on that side. Dipped down low I slowly walked to the edge of the driveway farthest away from the yard and crept up. When I got up to the house, I checked the corners and sho nuff he had cameras and also motion light sensors. I sat there and thought about what I wanted to do. I was going to have to do this the other way by knocking on this nigga door and hoping he let me in.

I made my way over to the front porch avoiding the camera and rang his doorbell. I looked over my shoulders at the sound of a car driving by. I could hear him walking to the door, but he never said who is it. His big ass is probably paranoid.

"Who is it?" he finally asked.

"Synzari," I answered.

I could hear the locks being undone. He opened the door and stood there looking at me up and down. I couldn't hold it in, so I laughed at this nigga.

"What you want, nigga?" he barked. I leaned back as if I was offended.

"I came over here to talk to you about your sister. What's with the hostility?" I asked. Kalicio crossed his arms as if he wasn't about to let me in.

"What you need to talk to me about?" he questioned. Thinking fast, I had to say something to get him to let me in this house.

"I understand that you're the only family, well man in Kali's life and I want to get your blessing to date her," I lied. I knew damn well him and Kali were beefing hard and she didn't give a damn what he thought. He chuckled and moved to the side letting me in. Kalicio closed the door and led me the living room. I took a seat on the sofa.

"You want something to drink?" he asked. I shook my head no. I didn't have time for no drink I needed to remain focused on the task at hand.

"So you call yourself really like Kali? She ain't run you away yet with her bossy ways?" he asked with a smug look on his face. I could tell he was one of them *talk about you like a dog behind ya back* types.

"Yeah, I really like her. Kali and I vibe well off of each other, and she actually lets me be the man," I threw that shade out there for him to catch. I pulled my phone out and looked at it pressing a few buttons then I placed it back in my pocket.

"Why you hate your sister so much?" I just came out and asked. The way he was looking at me, I could tell he was questioning my question.

"What makes you think I hate my sister? That's my sister, flesh and blood," he had the nerve to say. This nigga was funny.

"Your flesh and blood, huh? From what I was told, she practically raised you and looked out for you. She even put you in a position to get paid because that's what family do. Then to see the shit that you been doing to her is fucked up, my nigga," I said. Kalicio leaned forward.

"Nigga, what is you getting at? I don't know what the hell KK done told you, but I ain't did shit to her. That little shit that happened at the meeting was nothing. She accused me of some foul shit!" he yelled.

"She didn't even accuse you of what you actually did. She's running round here trying to figure out why motherfuckers are dropping and who doing this to her when the whole time it's been her brother bringing heat," I told him.

"I don't know what the hell you talking about, and I think you need to leave coming up in my house accusing me of shit. Wait until I tell Kali," he had the nerve to say.

"Kalicio cut the bullshit, my nigga. Damn, you already caught so you might as well tell the truth, or do you want me to tell it for you, my nigga? You bitch made, and it's fucked up that you used Kali name to help you get plugged in with Premium. What's even more fucked up is you used your sister's business that she built by giving Premium that fake ass batch of money. Who you think found out the money was fake? That was all me. This nigga done put a hit out on you and your sister. Your sister's walking around here clueless because she doesn't know it's a hit on her head due to her dumb ass brother putting her name in shit. You a snake ass nigga," I said calmly.

"Man, fuck you. You don't know what's it like to be raised under her. Yeah, she meant well, and she did what she was supposed to do being the oldest. However, she ain't respect me. Respect goes a long way and every chance she got, she's belittled me in front of people making them lose respect for me. That shit I did with Premium I wasn't expecting for it to come back like that," he said.

This man was a trip.

"You keep talking bout respect this and respect that, but you used the one person you didn't respect to get put on. You know why? Because people respect Kali. Her name is respected, and her name got you plugged in," I told him just in case he forgot.

"So, what you gone tell Kali? She ain't going to believe you. It's your word against mine." He laughed. I turned around so that I could leave.

"You won't be able to tell your side." I laughed.

When I turned back around, he didn't even have time to see the gun I shot him in between the eyes twice, and his body went flying back in the chair he was sitting in. I walked over to him and watched as the blood poured from his head and mouth. Kalicio was a big nigga so watching him squirm I was waiting on him to take his last breath. I checked my pocket and turned the recorder off. I had made sure I taped the conversation of his admittance so that I could let Premium know the details because I wasn't killing Kali, and I don't care what the hell he said. Looking back over at Kalicio he finally stopped moving. I bent down and checked his pulse, and he was gone. With my work done, I placed my gun back in my pants and pulled my hood back over my head. I used my sleeve to open the door and walked back down the driveway to my car. I didn't want to get caught running, and someone saw me. When I got back to my car, I hopped in and pulled off.

I sent Premium a text that Kalicio had been handled. I didn't feel bad for what I did I just felt bad for how Kali would take it. I couldn't call her because I was supposed to be out of town, I headed to the hotel that I was staying at deciding I would take it in for the night and wait for the news to unravel.

KALI

I had dozed off last night between calling Myia and Kalicio, but nobody was answering their phone. This wasn't like Myia, and I couldn't figure out why she wasn't answering. Now Kalicio, as much as I blew his phone up, I figured he would've eventually answered. With him not answering either, I started to get concerned. This morning soon as I woke up, I tried calling both again, and now Kalicio phone was going straight to voicemail. After I got dressed and had Marisol make me the strongest coffee, I headed out to my brother's house.

The entire drive I drove in silence. For some reason, I was trying not to think the worst, but I couldn't help it. My nerves were getting the best of me. That damn coffee I had was not sitting right on my stomach. With all the stuff that was happening lately, I prayed to God that nothing had happened to my brother and Myia. Of course, my security wasn't far behind. I turned into the driveway and parked behind Kalicio's truck. Myia's car wasn't here. Where the fuck was this girl at? Getting out the car, I turned around and waited until my guys got out and accompanied me. When everyone was here, I headed up the steps and got ready to knock on the door. When I got ready to knock security pulled my hand back and shook his head.

"The door is opened," he said and pointed to the crack door.

Looking down at the knob, it was slightly cracked. Security stepped in front of me and pulled out his gun while the other guy followed behind him doing the same.

"Stay here and let us go check everything out first," he said. Nodding my head, I stood on the porch and held myself.

I felt a panic attack coming on because now I was more scared than ever. It felt like time was moving slow, and I continued to pace back and forth. One of my guys made his way back on the porch, and the look on his face didn't sit well with me.

"What is it?" I asked. He looked down then back over his shoulder. That was it. I couldn't take this shit no more. I pushed passed him and headed into the house. When I rounded the corner, I saw my other security on the phone standing over my brother's body.

"Oh my god!" I yelled out, covering my mouth. I walked over to Kalicio's body shaking my head. I couldn't believe someone had done this to my brother. I dropped to my knees, and the tears started to fall.

"Come on, Kali. Get up so that you don't get any blood on you. I called the police they should be here any second," he told me helping me off the floor. I sat on the couch and just stared at my brother. Somebody had shot my baby in his head. This shit just kept on happening.

"I check the entire house, and it was clear nothing seems to be missing or out of place. If I know anything from the way this looks, he let the person inside. It's no forced entry," he told me.

I knew me and my brother was butting heads right now, but this shit wasn't cool. I grabbed my phone and called Myia again. It was some shit going on. She didn't answer again, so I sent her a text.

Me: Myia you need to call me or get home ASAP it's about Kalicio!!

Myia had better hope she ain't have nothing to do with my brother's murder. Nah, she wasn't that type of person, and I know she loved my brother. I could hear the sirens near and just sat there continuing to stare at my brother. The officers came in and immediately tried to remove me from the scene, but my feet felt like concrete blocks were attached to them. Once on the porch, I sat there in tears as my security detail explained to them the what had taken place.

"Ms. Kusain, we are sorry about your brother's murder. We are going to do everything we can to get to the bottom of this. Here is my card, and you can call me if you have any questions or leads," the officer told me.

All I did was shake my head. I wasn't interested in calling no damn officer if I found out anything. You bets believe this was going to be handled the best way and that was in the streets.

We had been here I know for about an hour, and they were still processing the scene. I looked up at the sky then turned around because I heard the front door open. The coroner was bringing my brother body out the house. That's when it hit me that Kalicio Kusain my only brother was gone. It took about four of them to carry the gurney because of how big my brother was. When they hit the bottom step, they let the wheels down and rolled him in front of me. I reached out and touched the body bag, and again I broke down. I didn't even get to tell him I loved him and that I was sorry about everything. He left this world thinking that I possibly didn't love him and we were beefing. Things weren't supposed to go that way.

A loud scream caused me to turn around at a screaming Myia making her way up the driveway. I got up to meet her and try to get her to calm down.

"What happened?" she screamed as she fought and literally grabbed Kalicio's body while on the stretcher.

"Ma'am, you're going to have to let us put him in the truck," one of the officers tried to tell her. When I got to her, she looked at me and fell in my arms. I held her, and we cried together.

"What happened to him, KK?" she asked. I grabbed her hand and led her out of the way of the officers.

"When we got here, the door was open, and they found him like that, shot twice in the head. I had come over because I'd been blowing the both of you up and wasn't getting no answer. What the hell is going on with you, Myia? You didn't show to work and are dodging everybody calls." I switched over from calm to angry. I could hear my voice change.

"KK, I left Kalicio's ass yesterday. We got into a fight when we got home, and I packed up my shit and left. I wasn't answering no calls because I needed to get away and clear my head," she cried.

We were going to talk about this some more, but right now, my mind couldn't process all this shit.

* * *

AFTER THE POLICE were done and finally gone. Myia and I had gone inside the house. She stood there staring at the blood-soaked chair and carpet where my brother laid and died.

"I have to get someone here to clean this," she rambled. She started walking around, and all I could do was think about that it was somebody that Kalicio knew or let in the house because he knew.

"Myia I need to know what happened between you and my brother," I voiced just as calmly as I could. Myia looked at me like I had two heads.

"What exactly are you trying to say, KK?" she yelled. Now me and Myia both didn't play, and I know she wasn't scared of me, but I was questioning shit.

"What I'm trying to say is you telling me you and Kalicio got into it then you left. No one was able to get in contact with you. Then my brother turns up dead. Somebody that he knew did this!" I spat.

"KK, you sound like a fucking fool. First of all, I may have punched his ass here and there over the course of our relationship, but this shit ain't me, no matter the issue between the two of us. I wouldn't do nothing of this magnitude. Despite the things he did, I still loved him. Plus my ass wouldn't come back here. I would've been long gone by now. You and your brother took me in and treated me like family. I have always been loyal to y'all, so me killing Kalicio is not my cup of tea!" Myia yelled.

She made sense. I was going to find out who killed my brother.

MYIA

I didn't know how long I was going to be able to ignore KK because she kept calling and blowing up my phone. However, when I read her text, I took my ass to the house Kalicio and I shared fast as hell, but I wasn't expecting to see what I saw at all. The one man that I loved was gone. The fact that Kali had the nerve to accuse me or even question if I had something to do with his murder was beyond me. I mean I could see the suspicion that she may have gathered from me, but I would never. Nevertheless, I knew who was behind it, and this had Premium's name all on it. I needed to tell Kali what was going on because I knew she was next.

From the eerie feeling that this house gave me, I knew that I wasn't going to be able to live here anymore. The news crew had been here and left so now the word was out thanks to the media that he had been murdered. I slowly walked down the hall to his office and pushed the door opened. His cologne still lingered in the room. I walked over to his chair and took a seat at his desk. Using my finger, I traced the oak wood just touching it thinking of him sitting behind here barking orders or hearing his loud, boisterous laugh bounce off the walls. I felt the tears start to flow again.

I pushed the mouse out the way, and the computer flashed on. The cameras were up from the house I could see KK still sitting in the living room and of course the different places the cameras were on outside. I clicked on the living room camera and went down the timeline to see if I saw anything from Kalicio's murder.

I watched the cameras and was going back until I saw some figures on one video. I paused the video, and this damn camera was positioned in the dumbest way. I could see Kalicio sitting on the couch, and I could tell that he was talking to somebody. He stayed that way for a little bit, and then you see him stand up. Whoever he was talking to he didn't feel threatened by because he looked calm the entire time. I jumped back in my chair at Kalicio being struck in the head by the bullet. He went flying back in the chair. I tried to quickly check the outside camera, but it was so dark and whoever left out the house was dressed in all black and was hiding from the camera leaving us nothing to make out.

"What are you looking at?" KK came walking into the room. I wiped my eyes and shook my head.

"The cameras, whoever came in here Kalicio didn't fear them, and he knew them. He was comfortable on the video talking to whoever it was. Look at this," I told Kali going back to the video. Kali walked over to me and watched the video. She held her head down watching Kalicio get shot.

"What did the outside cameras show?" she asked.

"Nothing, they kept away and shielded from the cameras," I told her.

"I want to have him buried quickly. I don't want to sit around on this because I'm leaving to go to Peru for a while. You were his woman, so you have the say on how you want everything. I still have to process all this and try to find out who the hell did this," she whispered. I felt so bad, and I was trying to build the courage up to tell her.

"Kali," I said. Kali turned to look at me.

"I want to go with you, I need to get away and clear my head," I told her. She shrugged her shoulders.

"I don't care. I can get Canton to look over everything while we gone," she spoke. It was now or never, and I wasn't sure how this was going to go, but I had to tell her.

"KK, I need to tell you something," I said nervously.

"Oh really?" she asked. I could tell she was thinking crazy already.

"The real reason why Kalicio and I broke up was because I found out some shit that I couldn't accept. I should've told you as soon as I found out, but I was leaving that to him. The only thing I didn't know he would never live to tell you. When we got home yesterday, I went to fix him, something to eat and he came into the office. He was on a phone call when I brought the plate to him, so I sort of eavesdropped. I heard him telling whoever was on the other end about giving a fake batch to Premium as payment for the drugs he received. Not only that, but he used your name to get plugged in. He knew that Premium had a price on both of your heads and that's who had something to do with Chris and MJ's murder. So I'm guessing whoever came here was either Premium or somebody else that Kalicio knew," I admitted. KK stood there speechless, and she grabbed her chest and took a seat.

"Myia, please tell me you lying? I can't see Kalicio doing this." She shook her head.

"KK, I wish. We had fallen out that time he had me make the batch. He told me Premium ordered a quick batch, and he needed it asap. I didn't think he was using it to pay him. It was something wrong with your brother. Like I have never seen him despise you the way he did. It was as if he didn't care or even try to justify what he was doing. He made it out like you just didn't treat him the way he should have. Like I told him, you don't like your sister yet you use her name as clout to get what you need. He wasn't trying to hear that from me, and he swore that I was trying to kiss your ass. So, I packed a few things and left. I couldn't face you just yet because he was the one that needed to tell you what he did," I cried.

I think I was crying tears of freedom because telling KK I felt like a weight had been lifted off of me

"So, this nigga Premium's been behind this the whole time. He just doesn't know what he has started," she said.

KYEATE

I watched as KK pulled out her phone. This shit was about to get ugly.

KALI

Watching that video and seeing my brother gunned down like that fucked me up, but what fucked me up more was the bomb that Myia just dropped on me. Premium was going to pay since he wanted to play. He just didn't know I could play the game just as well. I placed a call to my crew and put them up on game. I didn't want Premium dead yet, but he was going to feel my pain. I didn't care if his granddaddy got caught in the crossfire.

I sat and thought about everything that Myia had told me and how he used my name to get plugged in. Kalicio used my profit that he knew was against my rules. This entire time the snake was slithering around me. I thought back to that night that Syn and I were talking, and he asked me how I would react if I found out my brother was behind this shit. This was the reason why Kalicio acted an ass at the meeting because he was close to be outed. Now with the truth out, I didn't know how I felt. I wanted Premium for coming after me, and I felt Kalicio just got what he had coming to him. Karma was a bitch, but I do wish my brother were still alive so that I could confront him about this shit.

When I got home, Marisol met me at the door, and she threw her arms around me.

"Oh, sweet baby, I'm sorry about your brother. I saw it on the news. Are you okay?" she asked. I appreciated Marisol so much. I gave her a small smile.

"I'm fine thanks for asking. I just want to shower and go to bed. Myia and I must meet with the funeral people tomorrow." I sighed.

"I understand. If you need anything, just buzz," she told me.

Dragging myself upstairs, I headed to my room. I kicked my shoes off at the door and threw my purse in the chair. Plopping down on the bed, I fell back and stared at the ceiling. My phone was going off constantly, and I wasn't answering texts or calls because I didn't want to hear no more I'm sorry and condolences. I knew that Syn was working, but I wanted to hear his voice more than anything. I could at least try. I reached for my phone and dialed Syn number. The phone rang a few times, and to my surprise, he answered.

"Hello." His voice sounded so good.

"Hey, I'm sorry to call because I know you were working, but I had to hear your voice," I said I know he heard my voice crack.

"What's wrong, baby? You good?" he asked.

"No, I'm not good. My brother was murdered today," I cried.

"Oh, damn wow, you serious?" he asked.

"Yes, my security found him. Then on top of that, Myia told me what he did. He was the one that was bringing the heat to me. He had given Premium a fake batch of bills for drugs and used my name, so this whole time it's been Premium doing all this. I know that you work under him sometimes, but did you know anything about this?" I asked.

"Just what you told me today. Besides work, Premium and I don't work like that," he said.

"But ain't you a shooter or some sort?" I knew I was wrong for saying that shit over the phone I smacked my head after I asked that.

"Really Kali? Look, I'm sorry about your brother, and I'm not sure what you're getting at, but you should know how one operates on phones, baby girl. I'll hit you when I get back in town," he said.

"Yeah, I'm sorry. I'll talk to you when you get back," I told him and ended the call.

I headed to my closet, reached on the top shelf, and pulled a book down. Walking back over to the bed, I sat down and opened it. The pages were filled with pictures of Kalicio and me when we were little up until teenagers. The smiles that graced our faces you wouldn't have never thought that we would get to this point. I was just having the hardest time accepting the why.

Synzari

I DIDN'T WANT to answer the phone for Kali, but I knew why she was calling. Of course, I had seen the news, and I knew very well why she was calling. Kali was asking things that I wasn't about to answer over the phone, and I was shocked that she even said that shit. This shit was going to be harder than I thought because now she knew why Premium had Kalicio killed. However, once she found out I did that shit, I don't know how she was going to take it. A nigga had fucked up in a major way, but my job was my job. That nigga had that shit coming. I hated to lose Kali behind this, but if that what was going to happen, then I couldn't control it and I wasn't going out without a fight though.

I didn't want to be seen in town tonight, but this was a Gran Mae kind of night. I needed to be up under her wisdom and love right now. I had gotten rid of everything that I wore to Kalicio's house and grabbed my bag and hotel key.

KALI

Three days had passed since my brother's death, and it was time to bury him. Myia had planned everything. I just paid for it. I still was uneasy about everything. Yeah, this was my brother, but I was salty as hell. I felt like doing him like they did dude in the movie *CB4* and punching the hell out of dude in his casket. We were in the limo headed to the church, and everyone was dressed in black and mourning. I was dressed in a bright red Dolce & Gabbana pants suit and huge shades to cover my eyes. Myia leaned over and whispered in my ear.

"I can't believe you wore that shit for real," she said.

"I'm just showing my anger. I'm sure where Kalicio is going they wear red in hell right," I whispered back. I don't know what stage of grief I was at because I went from missing him and reminiscing to wanting to kick his ass. I felt I was the only one that could do that though. Was I wrong because he was dead? How was I supposed to act? Every time I think about somebody actually out here looking to kill me right now, I just get mad all over.

When we arrived at the church all these damn people who probably didn't even fuck with my brother was lined up outside. Security escorted us out of the limo and into the church. Stepping into the church, it was filled to capacity. Some faces I recognized, some I didn't. I had done business with a few people.

Myia and I walked up to Kalicio's casket. He was dressed in all white. My brother wasn't a suit wearing type of nigga, so Myia had him in some white Balmain jeans with a white and gold Balmain trim shirt. His chains hung around his neck, and he looked so peaceful. His beard was perfect, and he almost looked as if he was sleeping. You couldn't even tell he got shot in the head. I rubbed Myia's back as she let out her tears. After a few minutes, she got herself together, and we took our seats on the front row. I sat somewhat sideways on the pew so that I could see who all was walking down the aisle. Even though I had security in this bitch so deep, people were in here that I didn't know, and Premium could've hired anybody to do the job.

I looked over my shades as the girl that Kalicio was messing with that night Myia showed her ass in the club made her way down the aisle. Myia wasn't paying attention and I just shook my head. When Myia finally looked up at the casket, this girl was laid all over Kalicio crying and shit. I could feel Myia get tense, so I grabbed her arm.

"Fuck that, KK. This hoe ain't finna disrespect ever again," she said. Myia stood up and walked up to the casket. I quickly followed.

"You gone have to take that shit up out of here, July. Don't make me beat your ass," Myia said low enough for just us to hear. Then that's when it clicked in me that this bitch was Premium's sister.

"Bitch this is a funeral, and you can't control who comes and pay their respect!" she yelled. Everyone in the church gasped, and I stood there with my arms crossed.

"Let me tell you something really quick before I beat your ass. This here I paid for. So, I can put out whoever the fuck I want. If you don't take your thot ass up out of here, I promise you, you finna be laying up here next!" Myia spat.

July adjusted her dress, which looked like something she should've worn to the club the night before. I signaled for a couple of my guys to come and escort her. They grabbed her, and I held up my hand for them to wait. I stood in July face, and I grabbed this cheap ass rug she had hanging from her head pulling her face towards mine.

"I have a message that I want you to give your brother. You tell him Kali said I'm coming for him," I whispered.

I shoved her head back and shooed my hand signaling for them to remove this bitch. She caused a scene the whole way out of the church. We walked back and took our seats, and Myia was on ten.

"This nigga dead and gone and I still got to deal with these hoes." She chuckled. I don't think she was laughing because it was funny though. They continued with the service as if nothing happened.

This nigga funeral was so damn long. I don't know why Myia had all these fools talking. Damn, I thought Aretha's funeral was long. My stomach was growling, and I had an attitude out of this world. Then the time I was dreading came. They wanted me to address the congregation. I walked up to the podium. I cleared my throat and adjusted the mic.

"Thank you all for coming out and paying your respects to my brother. I didn't write no long drawn out speech. I'm not even going to get up here and lie. What I will say is that we were all each other had family wise. I raised my brother, took him up under my wing, and made sure he was straight. Yes, I love my brother. I even loved him when he said the most hurtful things to me. I'm lost with my feelings because I'm angry from being betrayed, and I'm hurt from being lied to. I hate that just the day before we had gotten into a heated argument. I feel like we would've gone weeks or maybe months without talking before one of us broke the ice from missing the other so much. But now, that can't happen because he's gone. So, I can't pop him in the head and do all the things a big sister would do. I have sat here all cried out because I have passed that stage. I'm just so angry, but I know that one day I will slowly heal from this. He is still my brother, and I am still my brother's keeper. With that being said I love you Kalicio, even though I'm so mad at you." I ended my speech there and made my way back to my seat. Myia squeezed my hand.

"That was good how you worded that and was able to express your feelings. I'm proud of you, KK," she said.

* * *

After the funeral, we stood around outside. My brother wasn't going to be buried. He was getting cremated. I had told Myia before that I was going to Peru. I just didn't tell her when. I was leaving today.

"Myia I have to get to the airport. The jet is waiting. I'm leaving today because shit is about to get real. I mean really real," I told her.

"I told you I wanted to come with you," she whined.

"I suggest you come on because I'm leaving now," I told her. Myia didn't seem to think long about it.

"Let me go talk to the funeral director about your brother's ashes. I watched as she ran off and I headed towards the limo. Once the door was opened, I climbed inside. I needed a drink, so I grabbed me a glass and cracked open the bottle of champagne that sat back there. I cleaned the glass in one sip. The door opened, and Myia climbed in.

"They're going to hold him until I get back," she said.

"Why are you keeping his ashes?" I asked.

"KK, even though y'all were at odds, he was still the man I loved. He was still the man that got me up out that strip club."

"I got you up out that strip club," I interrupted.

"You helped him, but I left because of him. He was all I knew. I don't feel right abandoning him. You're just angry right now. Pour me a glass," she asked. I poured her a glass of wine.

"So, you ready to see a whole new side of the world?" I asked Myia.

"Anything is better than here right now. Wait, have you talked to Syn?" she asked.

Shaking my head no, I felt my heart start to hurt. I hadn't talked to him since that night we got off the phone when I asked him about Premium. I missed him so bad, but right now getting away was more important than sitting around waiting on my demise.

KALI

Lima, Peru

I had slept most of the eight-hour flight to Peru. I didn't realize how tired I was, but I guess after the last few days I've had, sleep didn't come easy. We had just landed at Jorge Chavez International, and My cousins were waiting when we got off the jet. We both didn't have nothing but the clothes on our back. That was nothing a little shopping couldn't handle. My cousin Gustavo stood there with his arms wide.

"Kali!" he yelled.

It was nice to see him, and I fell into his embrace. Gustavo was talking Spanish to one of his guys that was standing to the side. I spoke a little, but I hated when it was spoke around me.

"Gus, you know I ain't with that shit," I told him. He let out a laugh.

"I am sorry, beloved. He doesn't speak English at all," he told me. We walked through the airport and headed to his car.

"I'm so sorry about Kalicio. I hate that you guys had to go through that," he said. I had told Gustavo about everything, so he was up to speed with everything that happened.

"It's ok. I'm just taking it a day at a time. This is Myia though. Kalicio's girlfriend and my other business partner," I told him. He lifted her hand and placed a kiss on it.

"My condolences," he told her. Once we were settled in the car, Gus looked at me.

"So where are you staying? You know I have plenty of room at the estate for you and your guest," he asked.

"We're at the Belmond Miraflores Park," I said, looking at the reservation on my phone.

"Oh, I forgot you bougie," he said, starting the car. I had to laugh.

"Gus, I know you mean well, but I came here to get away from all the violence. You the only nigga I know who got a mansion in the middle of the hood. I ain't got time for no gang shit," I admitted.

"My shit is guarded, and nobody knows not to cross the gun line with no shit. Ain't nothing wrong with living in the hood. How long you staying anyways?" he asked.

"I really don't know. I'm just taking it day by day," I honestly said.

"Well, it's all good. You know if you need anything, I'm just a phone call away, and if I need to send my guys to the states, I can do that too," Gus stated.

I knew that if he did that it wasn't going to be a pretty sight. I nodded my head and continued to look out the window at the beautiful scenery.

* * *

Forty-five minutes later, we pulled up at the hotel I couldn't wait to check in and head to the mall.

"Thanks for the ride Gus, make sure you let me know when the meeting is so that I can be there," I told him. Gus kissed my cheek and Myia, and I got out of the car.

"Ohh KK, this is beautiful," she gleamed. Belmond was beautiful, and it was right beside the Pacific Ocean.

We entered the hotel and checked in at the front desk. After receiving our keys, we were lead to our suite by the concierge. I was laughing on the inside because you would think Myia ass ain't ever been nowhere. The concierge let us in the room. This suite was everything and was two bedrooms so Myia and I would have our own side. The huge glass doors that led out on to the patio overlooked the swimming pool and the Pacific. This was the type of peace that I needed in my life. Nothing could be heard but the sounds of the water.

My phone started ringing, and it was Syn. I just looked at his name on the screen.

"Why are you ignoring him, KK?" Myia asked.

"I just don't want to talk to him. I'm slick embarrassed at how I came at him about Kalicio's death," I admitted.

"Syn is understanding and apparently he's not fucked up with it because he keeps calling you," she said. I couldn't be anything for Syn right now.

"Look I don't know how long I'm staying here and right now I can't deal with all that relationship type shit clouding my judgment!" I yelled. I was done having this damn conversation. "Let's head to the mall!" I told Myia.

Whenever I came here, I always hit up Lacomar. It was my go-to shopping spot, and if I wanted American food like Burger King or Starbucks, this was the spot.

Myia

When we arrived here, my breath was taken away because I never knew Peru was this pretty, well this side. Kalicio would talk about it and sometimes Kali, but they would always just talk about when they came up here and the part of Peru they grew up in. I assume that's why she didn't want to stay at Gus place because I heard her say it was in the hood. I wasn't complaining about where we stayed. I was just blessed to be here. Right now, all we had were each other. I know Kali wouldn't talk much about Syn or her brother, but I knew she was dealing with those demons.

Retail therapy was exactly how she was handling that. On top of us coming here with nothing, we had a lot of shopping to do. We were here in the M.A.C store getting a few things. A girl was nothing without her makeup. I had grabbed my favorites while Kali was purchasing what she needed. I noticed she used cash, which was something that she rarely did. When we walked out of the store, I pulled Kali to the side.

"When did you start using cash?" I whispered.

"I have to get rid of some of this. Girl, now you know this is where all the magic happens. My cousin is so cold at this shit here that it isn't detected, period. So I'm going to spend what I can. Ain't no point in holding on to it," she said.

Now back home we didn't spend the shit. We just made it and gave it to whoever ordered it. I wasn't trying to come all the way to Peru and get locked up. Kali handed me some money.

"Here go buy you something. It's all good Myia, I promise," she said.

I was hesitant at first, but once I made it out the first store undetected, after that it was a wrap. KK and I had bought so much stuff that we had to send shit back to the hotel because we couldn't carry it all by ourselves. We ended our shopping trip with some really good Peruvian food. So far, things were going good, and I prayed that they stayed that way.

SYNZARI

I had been at Gran Mae's for a few days, longer than I intended on staying the first time. A nigga was going through the motions, and I didn't like this feeling. I had tried calling Kali because I wanted to check on her after her brother's funeral to see how she was holding up, but she wasn't answering a nigga calls. That led me to believe she was mad about something. I was worried if she had believed that I had something to do with Kalicio's death because of the shit she asked me. I wanted to tell her the truth, which I had planned on it, but the shit that she was saying over the phone, she knew that wasn't proper. I didn't trust for a lot of things to be said over the line, so I ended the convo before it got too deep. Yeah, I lied to her, but I couldn't tell her the truth right there like that. This was a conversation that needed to happen face to face.

I was propped up on the couch watching ESPN, and Gran Mae had just come in from some dance. I shook my head because her ass needed to sit down somewhere out here going to parties and shit. I could tell she had been drinking. She was still humming whatever tune she had in her head. She sat down in her chair and removed her shoes.

"Shit, my damn feet is killing me," she groaned and started to massage her feet.

"That's because your ass needs on some old lady shoes, out here dressing like some young girl!" I groaned.

"Boy shut your shit, I told your ass to come to our dance. It was nice. Nigga, just because I'm old don't mean I have to sit up and die. I'm living my damn life. What the hell done got into you, Latrell? This is the longest you done been here, and quite frankly you are getting on my damn nerves!" she yelled. When granny got riled up that shit was funny to me.

"Damn, I guess I go home then since I'm not welcomed," I joked

"I swear you ain't got the sense God gave you. You know I know when something wrong, so I got time tonight. I'm lit so tell me this shit," she said as she sat back in her chair and locked her fingers into each other resting her arms across her chest.

"You remember I was telling you about that little issue I was having with that girl? Well turns out she was innocent in the situation. We had been kicking it heavy then some things happen, and her brother got killed. She was taking it hard and sort of pushed me away. I'm not knowing how to deal with this."

I told her somewhat of the truth. In no way could I tell Gran Mae everything that went down because she would have a damn heart attack.

"Latrell, I feel you just gave me a washed-out version, but one thing you need to remember is that people grieve differently. You said yourself that things happened then her brother was killed, so maybe she's just dealing with all that. I say if you really like her just keep trying. She will see that someone is trying to be in her corner even though she isn't letting them. God has a funny way of doing things. Have you tried to go see her?" she asked.

"She just up and left after her brother funeral," I said.

"Oh, she doesn't want to be bothered period. I would tell you to move on, but I see your heart is with this one, and Latrell your heart ain't ever been with nobody." She smiled.

"This is why, shit like this," I admitted. I didn't like this feeling. The one time I give a bitch a chance she throws a nigga off his game.

My phone buzzed, and I grabbed it hoping it was Kali but that quickly faded when I saw Premium's name. On God, this nigga was irritating my soul. He was pressing the issue that I handle Kali because his sister came to him with a threat that Kali sent and shortly after one of his men was found dead. I smiled at the thought of Kali getting her vengeance. Premium really thought I was out here looking for her. I was but not to complete his failed ass mission. I wanted my Kali back for me and me only. I knew I was going to have to take Premium out when this was all said and done.

MYIA

We had been in Peru for two months now, and Kali had drugged herself into a deep depression. Now I could've sworn this trip was to the do the complete opposite. The first week everything seemed to go great, and we did a lot of sightseeing. She attended the meeting and then she just went downhill from there. All Kali was doing was eating and sleeping her life away. She would come out of the room to shower and take a swim, but I didn't know what was going on with her.

Canton and I had been communicating regarding everything that was going on back home. I figured with a lot of Premium's soldiers coming up dead that she would be happy, but she would just shrug it off. I had even tried to get her to call it off, but she wouldn't. This shit was starting to get boring. I was about to get things riled up in here because I was tired of this mopping around. I lightly tapped on Kali's door because I didn't know if she was sleeping or not.

"Come in!" she called out. Turning the knob, I opened the door and walked into the room Kali was coming out of the bathroom and starting to climb back in bed.

"I'm surprised your ass ain't got decubitus ulcers, from being in that fucking bed so long." I sighed.

"You're being extra Myia because I do get out of bed," she mumbled.

"What the fuck is wrong with you, KK? I'm tired of this shit and if you don't let me know wassup, I'm packing my shit and I heading back home. We supposed to be here enjoying ourselves to get away from the bullshit that's going on back home, but damn, what the hell happened to you?" I yelled, throwing my hands up.

"Myia, nothing is wrong," she said, lying once again.

"KK, I thought we were better than that? What is it? Maybe you need to talk to somebody other than me. Have you answered any of Syn's calls? That boy's been calling every day since we been here. Niggas don't do that," I told her.

At the mention of Syn's name, I watched Kali place her face in her hands and break down. I walked over to the bed.

"What is it Kali, please talk to me?" I pleaded. Kali was starting to hyperventilate.

"Calm down, Kali. Look at me and breathe with me. I placed my hand on her chest and did a few breathing exercises with her until she was back ok.

"Now, tell me what the problem is. I mentioned Syn, and you lost it," I demanded.

Kali lifted her head and reached into the bedside drawer. Whatever she grabbed I couldn't make out until she flung it at me. I looked down and picked up a fucking piss stick.

"KK, that's fucking trifling!" I said grossed out. I looked at the pregnancy test, and it read positive. I looked back at her with wide eyes.

"Oh my god, when did you find this out?" I yelled. I didn't know if I was happy or pissed.

"A month ago," she cried. I jumped up off the bed.

"A month, KK, damn you! When the hell were you going to say something, when you went in labor?" I shouted.

"Stop shouting Myia, damn. This shit is already fucked up," she cried.

"It's nothing fucked up about you being a mother. You have a man that's practically begging you to talk to him, whom I assume is the father of this child. I'm sure he will be glad to hear this from you. So how is this fucked up? You need to go back home and talk to that man," I told her keeping it real with her.

"I can't go back home right now with all this shit going on. Myia it's a fucking hit on my head, and I don't want to spend my entire pregnancy stressed out and looking over my shoulders every time I leave out. Me being here is protecting my baby right now," she said.

"You talking about being stressed out when you been sitting here for two months stressed and depressed. I understand your reason for protecting your baby, but you also know what you're doing isn't healthy for the baby either. You should at least let Syn know he is going to be a father," I suggested.

"I will let him know when the time is right. I'm still pretty much digesting this. You know I never pictured me being somebody's mother." She laughed. I couldn't picture that shit either, but it was all going to be ok and a great learning experience.

Kali

I knew something was up with me when I couldn't keep shit down. I love Peruvian food, but Lord every time I ate it, it made me sick. Then not to mention I was always tired. At first, I tried to blame it on the time change and shit, but the more I tried to ignore the shit, it wasn't going away. When I missed my cycle, I knew I was pregnant all along. I just didn't want to accept it.

The day I took the pregnancy test, and it came back positive it really hit me. I knew I was wrong for slipping in a depressive state. I wanted nothing more to go back home and be with Syn. I wanted to call him up and just apologize and tell him, hey we having a baby. I just couldn't bring myself to do it. I was so used to doing things on my own that I felt I was handling the situation the best I could. I didn't think Myia would get as upset as she did. I knew once she found out she would push the issue about him, so that's another reason why I kept it from her.

Both Myia and I just sat there staring at each other.

"You know now that you come have told me this, you need to find a doctor here and start getting some type of prenatal care at least until you get back home. We can't be out here and not getting no medical attention for my godchild." She smiled. I nodded my head.

"I'm already ten steps ahead of you. Gus gave me the number to one of the best OB doctors here. You know that nigga and his wife got about six damn kids." I laughed.

"So, you told that nigga Gus before you told me?" Myia asked.

"No, I told him I needed a female doctor while out here," Myia was so damn jealous.

"Well, you need to get on the phone and get some appointments set. Wow, I can't wait to find out what you having!" Myia jumped in excitement.

I rubbed my hand across my stomach and couldn't believe I was about to have a kid. It was a human being growing inside of me. Kalicio would trip out at this shit. It was moments like this I would have random thoughts about my brother. I had finally got over of being angry at him because what was done had been done and it sure wasn't no changing it. All I knew that if it were my time to go then no matter how much I tried to dodge it, it would still come for me. I just wanted to give my baby a chance at a decent life. The day that I tell Syn, I hope that he understands and still accepts me and the baby.

Synzari

Walking into the house, Gran Mae had threw down on breakfast. I walked over, kissed her on the cheek, and grabbed a piece of bacon off the plate.

"Morning, Gran Mae," I told her. I took a seat at the table and waited on her to finish.

"Don't give up on that girl," she said. I didn't know what the hell she was talking about.

"Huh?" I asked.

"That girl you were telling me about awhile back. Don't give up on her. Keep calling. I dreamed of fish last night," she said, walking over to the table to hand me a plate.

"What the hell does fish got to do with anything, granny?" I asked.

"Somebody is pregnant, and it sure as hell ain't me. That leaves you unless your mammy done went and got knocked up," she said. This shit was crazy, and all I could do was laugh. Old folks and they dreams and sayings.

"I don't know what the hell you laughing for. Watch what I tell you. I'm finna have me a grandbaby, and it's about damn time," she said to herself and went to fix her a plate.

All I know is Kali motherfucking ass bet not be pregnant and keep that shit away from me.

KALI

SIX MONTHS LATER

When I pulled up at Synzari's house, I thought about how wrong I was to pop up here. Not talking to him for eight months was the hardest thing I had done. It was so much bloodshed while I was in Peru that it was best that I stayed away because I couldn't afford to risk my life. All the things that had happened I couldn't believe that I had even come back here period. Myia had insisted she came over her with me, but I dropped her off at the house. This was something that I had to do on my own. The entire plane ride I had played out how this would go and how I would tell him everything. It was now or never and time to face the music.

My security had driven me because I had been having pains and shit lately and I didn't want to chance anything by getting behind the wheel of a car. When I stepped out of the car, I tighten the strap on my coat. When Synzari told me that he didn't bring people to his house, I felt this was the reason why motherfuckers popping up when they wanted to. Syn had continued to call me every day, and I could've told him I was coming, but I didn't want nobody knowing that I was back in town yet. Walking towards the house, the jitters in my stomach were already telling me this might not be a good idea. I was afraid of rejection that may follow.

I slowly climbed the steps, and I stood there on the porch for a few seconds. The knots in my stomach got tighter. Letting out a huge sigh, I pressed the doorbell. I stepped back and prayed like hell some hoe didn't come to the door. The door flew open, and all I could do was smile, even though the look on Syn face wasn't a pleasant one. *Please say something.*

"Kali," he mumbled.

"Hi," was all I could muster up. He scratched his head and stepped out on the porch.

"Hi, is that all you have to say? It's been what eight months and I haven't seen or heard from you!" he spat. He was so close that I could've sworn I felt spit smacking me in the face. I wiped my face.

"Can I please come in? I can explain," I asked.

Syn smacked his lips and turned to walk back in the house, and I followed behind him. We stood in the foyer. He wouldn't even allow me all the way in the house.

"Explain!" he spat.

His voice was so cold. How could someone that called everyday act so cold when he finally sees me? I was expecting maybe some open arms or an *oh I missed you* type of welcome.

"I had to leave Syn, and you know why. Things were just too hot here, but I'm back now," I cried. My fucking hormones were all messed up. This damn baby was killing me.

"You were gone for eight whole months what the hell you come back for now and why you come here of all places. You hurt me Kali!" he yelled.

"Stop yelling at me. I came back because of this. Your daughter will be here soon, and she needs her father!" I yelled as I undid the belt on my coat exposing my protruding belly. I wasn't huge to be thirty-five weeks because I was carrying her in my hip and ass. So, the coat I wore had did a good job hiding my belly. Syn stood there with a confused look on his face.

"I found out I was pregnant when I got to Peru. The only reason why I didn't come back was because I didn't want to chance it. I should've called, but after the last convo we had, I just figured that things went all wrong," I admitted.

Syn began to pace the floor, and then he looked at my stomach.

"My granny told me that you were pregnant. She dreamed of fish. She told me not to give up on you. I wasn't going to let anything happen to you. I wasn't going to kill you," he mumbled. I wasn't sure if I heard that last part correctly.

"You weren't going to do what?" I asked.

"I said I wasn't going to kill you," he repeated.

I started shaking my head because I just know he wasn't referring to killing my brother. Was this nigga working for Premium the whole damn time?

"Did you kill my brother?" I asked. There was a clapping noise coming from the back and low and behold Premium entered the room.

"Oh yes, and now he can kill you," Premium laughed. I looked back and forth between Syn and Premium.

"Fuck you, Premium. You lucky you still standing!" I spat.

"Bitch, fuck you," Premium said. Why was everything happening to me?

"This whole time you were lying to me. I asked you about my brother, yet you acted like you ain't know nothing. You knew this whole time about everything from day one before I even knew what was going on. So, you feeling me and taking me out was that part of your job?" I yelled at Syn.

"Hell nah, I was feeling you way before this shit came about and before I even found out what your brother did. Even after the fact, I still wasn't finna do shit to you. I just couldn't tell you because brother or not, that nigga had to go for what he did. That nigga allowed motherfuckers to come for your whole crew. Blood don't do that shit. I was trying to prove to this nigga here that you ain't have nothing to do with that shit. Do you really think I would hurt you?" he asked.

"You hurt me by lying to me and keeping the truth from me," I cried.

"And if I had told you the truth, would you had been accepting of it, Kali?" Syn asked.

"Blah, blah, this hoe is guilty just like her brother," Premium spoke up.

"Shut the fuck up, nigga. I got proof that she ain't know what the hell was going on like I told you from the jump," Syn told Premium.

He pulled something from his pocket and soon I heard my brother's voice. It was he and Syn talking about the entire situation. Premium rocked a smug look on his face as if he was unbothered.

"It's too late for all that, Syn. You know this bitch done wiped most of my team out and even had somebody shoot up my granddaddy's restaurant, not to mention July getting shot at. She's got to go, and if you ain't gone be the one to do it, then I'm just gone have to do it myself!" Premium yelled, pulling his gun out and aiming it at me.

There was no way I walked in the house empty-handed. I reached behind my back and placed my hand on my gun pulling it out and aiming it at Premium. Here we were guns pointed at one another.

"Now nigga you know you ain't finna make it up out of here alive," Syn said and pulled his gun and had it aimed at the side of Premium's head.

"I guess we all about to be some shot up motherfuckers then," Premium laughed. This nigga was irking my soul.

"It ain't about to be too much talking, my nigga. You got like three seconds to put your gun down!" Syn called out. Premium slumped his shoulders as if he was disappointed.

"Aite man," he said

POW, POW, POW!

I dropped the gun and grabbed my neck as I hit the floor. I heard Syn yelling and rushing to my side.

"Fuck! Kali hold on!" he yelled.

All I could think about was my daughter. This nigga really shot me. I felt my chest on fire, and my neck was leaking. I didn't see any movement from Premium, so I knew he was dead. Syn came back and swooped me up. When he got out the door, he was yelling for help. I was trying to keep my eyes opened. I could hear my men screaming and asking what happened.

"Take care of my baby. Please save my baby," was all I could get out.

"Kali, man, stop talking and just hush. We're a block away from the hospital. You gone make it," he cried. I was trying to hold on for my baby. I quickly said a prayer.

"God, at this time I don't even care about my own life, but please don't take my innocent baby. Forgive me for all my sins."

I could hear Syn and a lot of people talking in the background, and I was fading in and out. The weaker I got, the less I heard. I wasn't sure if this was the end. Everything got dark, and maybe I was about to take my last breath because all the pain I ever felt had left my body. I couldn't feel anything. When I wake up, I will be able to hold my baby girl, hopefully. I hope God granted her life.

EPILOGUE

Sitting in front of the fireplace, I stared at the picture in the frame that I held. Staring back at me was the one that I would forever love. This shit had been so hard on me.

"Look, Kaliyah. you see mommy?" I whispered to my daughter. She was three months old, and I made sure every day I showed her who her mommy was.

Burying Kali had been the hardest thing I have ever done. That was some shit that I never saw happening in my life. I just couldn't wrap my head around loving someone but not being able to fully be with them. We never had the chance to see what we could've been. Even though I would've loved to be raising Kaliyah with Kali, I was thankful that my daughter survived. Kali was shot once in the chest and once in the neck. When she arrived at the hospital, the doctors were shocked that she held on as long as she did. They said she wasn't even supposed to hold on longer than ten minutes. I believe she was holding on for our daughter. Kaliyah was immediately removed from Kali via C-section.

Kali's death had hit everyone hard. Myia took it so hard. She had lost the two people that she considered family in a short period of time. Even through it all, she has been a big help with Kaliyah. Marisol didn't want to stop working even though I told her she could leave after we sold Kali's house. She wanted to be a part of Kaliyah's life also, so she was her nanny. My Gran Mae helped as much as she could, which made my heart melt. She finally got her wish of having a grandbaby, and Kaliyah was spoiled as hell. My ma even came back for a minute once she found out she had a granddaughter. I guess Kaliyah had a nice support system of women, but nothing would compare to Kali.

Being a father, I had to cut back on the shit that I was doing in the streets. I would forever be a shooter, but right now, I traded my guns for bottles and diapers. Canton and Myia tried to continue running Kali's business, but I shut that shit down for now. It was no need in being greedy because the money wasn't needed. I knew if Kali were still here, she would've been all about motherhood. Nobody was hurting for money. We all were just living and had made enough to do so. I sit and think about all the things that transpired and then look at where we are. When I feel my daughter squirm in my arms, my heart melts as it once did for her mother. I thank you, Kali, my queen, for leaving me with the next best thing.

The End For Now..

THANK YOU

Thank you so much for reading *Kali Kusain Counterfeit Queen*. This is book 17 for me, and I just thank all those that have supported me up until now. I like to thank all my new readers also for giving me a chance. I would appreciate if you leave a review on Amazon or Goodreads.

This year I have put a lot of stress on my body by trying to give you guys consistent drops. My last release *Tricked: A Halloween Love Story* was the book that got me the orange bestseller ribbon. I have felt the pressure of trying to make sure my work is better than the last. Sometimes we can be our toughest critics and not feel like what we do is good enough. I felt that with writing this book. I know each book from here on out I will feel that pressure.

I have one more release for you guys to end 2018 with a lovely bang. Next year I have a few things set up, but I also will take that time for myself that I need. Juggling a full-time job, mother of three kids, and trying to get you guys books every month catches up with you. So, next year I will try more quality over quantity. Mental health is very important. I deal with mental health issues, so I have to make sure I come first in everything. I love you guys and again thank you so much for reading.

KYEATE'S CATALOG

Take the time to read my catalog, and you will see my growth as a writer. The first three books were independent releases that I put out before I got signed to Mz. Lady P Presents. Then the rest are newer works since being signed.

Charisma vs. Cha Cha
    Deception: City of Lies
    Games He Play: Di'mond & Kyng

    A Savage and his Lady (Series) 1 & 2
    Masking My Pain
    Fiyah & Desire: Down to ride for a Boss
    Securing the Bag and His Heart (series)
    Securing the Bag and His Heart Too
    Remnants (Novella)
    5 Miles Until Empty (Novella)
    Once Upon a Hood Love: A Nashville Fairytale (Novella)
    Tricked: A Halloween Love Story (Novella)